CONCEIVED CHAOS

THE SELA HELSDATTER SAGA
BOOK TWO

RORI BLEU

ROSIE CHAPEL

First printing: 2023
ISBN: 978-0-6457084-7-9 (eBook)
ISBN: 978-0-6457084-8-6 (Paperback)

Ulfire Pty. Ltd.
P.O. Box 1481
South Perth
WA 6951
Australia

Cover Design: R Norman
Cover Image: Canva/Deposit Photos
Designed in Canva
Internal images: Canva/Deposit Photos.
Created using appropriate licences.

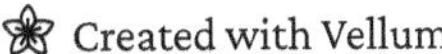 Created with Vellum

ACKNOWLEDGEMENT
RORI BLEU

Special thanks go out to my **Muse**, whose insistence on watching bad television, motivated me to do *anything* else to keep myself occupied!

ACKNOWLEDGEMENT
ROSIE CHAPEL

I am not sure Rori realises how felicitous was her request to collaborate in the revision of this incredible saga.
We *had* discussed the possibility on and off several times, but our schedules never seemed to coincide.
By accident... or, and as I prefer to think, fate... this time everything fell into place.
During the last eight months, for one reason or another, I have struggled to commit even a single sentence to paper, and had begun to question whether my muse had — quite thoughtlessly — abandoned me.
Working with Rori on Sela's story has re-kindled my inspiration and my motivation... for which, I shall remain forever grateful.

Thank you, my friend!

A NOTE FROM RORI

As with Book One, *The Flip of a Coin,* this story was written at the beginning of my career, and I wish to apologize for the immaturity of my writing style and composition.

I also wish to express my appreciation for the constant tutelage of my co-writer, Rosie Chapel. How she did not toss this trilogy into the trash, I'll never be sure.

If you have been tempted into re-reading the series, I hope you approve of this revised version.

If you are new to Sela's saga, I encourage you to immerse yourself in the second instalment of a thrilling story!

CONCEIVED CHAOS

The Sela Helsdatter Saga
Book Two

Rori Bleu

Rosie Chapel

PROLOGUE

The nightmare was always the same...

owling winds lash the weathered shingles of the sparsely populated tavern, relentlessly, as though Njord, himself, was trying to tear them off.

A young maiden moves from table to table, clearing the dirty dishes. Under her breath, she chastises the absent patrons for their messy eating habits.

Glancing at her swollen belly, she chuckles softly, watching the outline of tiny fists objecting to her working instead of resting as the healer had suggested.

Without warning, the door bursts open. An old woman is blown into the room and , except for the maiden, no one else seems to notice.

Although drenched — her clothes tattered and dirty, her hair matted from the storm — her eyes are ablaze with an implacable hatred which is directed at the maiden. Tears spill down her wrinkled cheeks as though she has been crying since birth.

The wizened crone screeches, "How dare you bear that bastard a child?"

As her screams reverberate around the tavern, the maiden realizes the life within her is no longer there...

ONE

J arred from sleep, Sela bolted upright.

Sobbing and shaking, she clutched her own swollen belly to convince herself it was just a dream. A stubborn kick provided the reassurance she needed, and allayed fears triggered by the nightmare.

Her lips curved as she watched the protestations of her unborn child at being so rudely awakened.

The life within her was definitely a product of the fiery couple who had conceived it.

That thought drained her smile, and she stared at the empty side of the bed.

Once more, Loki was gone.

While she had hoped it might be possible to change him, deep in her heart, Sela knew it was a futile wish.

Memories of their first few months together flickered through her mind like an old black and white movie.

Secret hours together until Thomas was able to resign his priesthood — to the simultaneous regret and happiness of his parish — and begin, to outward appearances, at least, his transition into Loki. Their *honeymoon* period, which started long before their wedding, had been idyllic.

Sharing innermost confidences. Something of their lives prior to their fated meeting.

Although aware of Sela's torment at Peer's hands, Loki knew little of her childhood and meteoric rise from peasant to ruler; intrigued and, if he was honest, a trifle intimidated by the story of her ruthless ascendance.

Sela pressed Loki on whether anything about his assumed persona was genuine, or simply a ruse to tug on her heartstrings. It transpired, Loki needed to vanish at the same time as he, coincidentally, overhead a certain Thomas Lockwood vowing to reform his life.

That he dispatched the man's soul to purgatory, before commandeering his physical form as a way to hide in plain sight, a happy accident, which worked in both their favours.

Sela blew a weighty sigh. Loki's love for her might be unequivocal, but it was *not* to the 'exclusion of all others' and, by 'others', she meant his fellow deities.

Was she being selfish, wanting her husband all to herself? She didn't think so and, to be fair... for the most part, he was. That didn't mean she had to *like* it when his role as a god interfered.

Sela had long wrestled with the question of how does one transform a god, especially one whose entire existence was the bane of Valhalla?

Each of the celebrated deities had a duty to perform, whether it be Odin's rule over gods and mortals, or the goddess Jörð's responsibility for Earth's care.

In Loki's case, no one knew what his role among the gods actually entailed, and he was not one to share.

Not even with the woman to whom he had pledged his love, and still leaves alone more times than I care to count.

His secretive nature ran counter to the rest of the gods and led to bitter conflicts. Nonetheless, time and again when the need arose, he was there to save them... to save **her**.

Was that where he had gone tonight? Sela knew Loki loved her, but was not convinced it was **only** her.

Perhaps Freya, the goddess who had toyed with Loki's heart for countless eons had stolen him away, or had fallen 'victim' to another insidious plot by the giants or fairies or...

Who the Helheim cares? Except, I'm sure whatever problem that whiny bitch managed to instigate, the love of my life was Johnny on the Spot to rescue her.

As much as she loved and respected Freya as a goddess, and sometimes irreplaceable friend, Sela cursed her hold over Loki and the cloud she had created over their marriage.

It was Freya who had broken the news to everybody, including Loki, that Sela was with child, before Sela herself was sure.

She made Freya swear to Odin that she would not reveal the sex of the babe because Sela did not want to know.

Grudgingly, Freya had agreed, but this did not stop her from dropping oblique hints.

"Bitch," Sela grumbled to the empty room.

She heard the click of the front door, followed by the thud of boots along the hall. Sela had no fear; she knew to whom they belonged.

If anything, it was the intruder who ought to be worrying, given he was about to be handed his head on a platter.

The instant the bedroom door opened, she groused, "You get lost on your way to the kitchen for your midnight snack? I hear breadcrumbs make a great trail guide. Oh, wait... that only works if you sweep up after yourself in the morning."

Sela jutted her chin out disdainfully, "Who am I kidding? It would be up to me to—"

Loki's exasperation cut her off, "Please, Sela, not tonight. I have neither the strength nor ambition to match your wit."

Sela felt the bed sag as he crumpled onto the edge of the mattress and, to her dismay, thought she heard him sobbing.

There were many facets to her husband, but for him to weep in front of her was something new... something disturbing.

Sela shuffled across to wrap her arms around his burly frame in an effort to comfort him. She sensed his body heaving ever-so slightly as she rested her chin on his shoulder.

She whispered in his ear, "Loki, *ástin mín*, my love, I was just kidding. What's the matter?"

He remained silent, collecting himself. "Sometimes, Sela what you consider amusing escapes me."

He paused to draw in a breath, as though hoping to avoid the next words.

"What is it, Loki?" Sela pressed, ignoring the trickle of ice slithering down her spine. Something was very wrong.

"We have to leave the city. Tonight. Right now." Loki could not face her.

"*Leave the city*? What in Odin's name for? I love this city and have no intention of leaving." Shocked, Sela pulled away, her tone adamant.

It had taken all her guile and charm to persuade Loki to stay in Manhattan after she had disposed of Peer.

There was nothing in Valhalla or on Midgard which could induce her to spend *any* time in Helheim, and even less desirous of enduring Loki's daughter's resentment over his decision to stay with a mortal.

Okay, Sela knew she could not quite classify herself as a mortal anymore.

A thousand years in Hell and the few *perks* Freya conferred upon Sela on her wedding day, before the two ceased talking to each other, had seen to that.

Oddly, of all the gifts in Sela's possession, the coin she had found when a child remained the most important. Freya had imbued the piece with a magic unknown within the realm of Midgard, transforming it into a talisman unlike any which preceded it.

Despite the subsequent animosity between the two, Sela wore the coin on a fine gold chain around her neck, and cherished the magic Freya had bestowed on her.

Neither had this amulet 'upgraded' Sela to the status of goddess, for which she was eternally grateful. They behaved like spoiled children, not omniscient beings charged with determining the fate of man.

Not the time to be dwelling on what she couldn't change. Sela dragged her mind back to what Loki was saying.

"There was a meeting called in the Hall this evening—"

Sela interrupted her unyielding god-husband, "And you didn't think to let me—"

Loki swung around, his eyes burning with the fires of Helheim.

"*Silence woman*," his command rattled the foundations of the building.

In all the time they had been together, Loki had never raised his voice to Sela. They argued with each other — they were both spirited individuals — there had even been a sword fight... or four, but not once had he spoken to her with such... wrath.

Wide-eyed and speechless, Sela sank back against the pillows.

"Bad enough I could not tell you or have you accompany me but, I was informed, had you done so, you would have been dead on arrival. You may not be able to die on Earth, Sela, but whatever magic transformed you into who you are now, is not enough to protect you in Valhalla."

Loki struggled to control his anger at his failure to keep Sela safe from the cretins who called themselves gods.

He knew everything was spinning out of control even as he tried to explain the facts to her.

"Who was at this family get-together?" Sela asked softly, mentally running down the list of likely suspects.

"All of the representatives from the nine worlds." Loki paused, and shook his head. "No, one of the realms was excluded."

Loki ticked off the culprits on his fingers, emphasizing the ominous nature of the situation.

"An ice creature of Niflheim, a fire being of Muspelheim. The entire Aesir tribe of Asgard, most wishing you had dared to put in appearance. One of the giants from Jotunheim, the Vanir tribe from Vanaheim, a couple of the elves of Alfheim, and the dwarf leader from Svartalfheim. Oh, and let's not forget..."

Loki paused for dramatic effect... as though that was in any way necessary.

"...my daughter Hel and her entourage from Helheim."

"How could I possibly forget your doting offspring? She'd rather see me crushed between two boulders for eternity instead of offering an affable *Hello*. Wait... Midgard was not invited?"

The absence of the representatives of Humanity, excluded from this meeting deliberately, concerned Sela.

"No, and while this confused me, Odin babbled on about why it did not affect them," Loki's ambivalence to the All-Father's decree, colored his response.

Sela tried to enclose Loki's massive paw in her small hand. Usually, the sight made Loki chuckle but tonight, with all the tenderness he could muster, he switched the gesture, engulfing her hand in his, instead.

"They want our child dead, Sela," Loki's words were as lifeless as the message they delivered.

Sela had already guessed the gravity of the matter, but this was something she could neither comprehend nor have foreseen.

"*D-Dead?*" she stammered her mind reeling. "*Why?* Our child is not yet born. How could it have committed any crime against the realms demanding this? It was that damned Freya's fault, wasn't it? Spilling the beans about our baby."

"Watch your tongue, Sela," Loki commanded, despite knowing full well Sela would not take a single iota of notice. "It's nothing Fr—"

"Oh, for Odin's sake," Sela stopped him mid-sentence. "You're seriously going to sit there and defend her? She's been haunting my dreams for the past three months. This has her fingerprints all over it."

"It's not about Freya," Loki refuted.

"Loki, I admire your loyalty... actually right now I don't... but you are deluded, if you think I'm going to let that witch harm our child. I'll kill her myself if I have to."

Loki hauled Sela into his lap.

She could feel his body trembling with suppressed rage. Tears welled in her eyes as she buried her face in his chest.

His fingers stroked through her hair, in a soothing motion. "It is because of what this child represents... to them. It is a danger to their entire existence. You know what kind of children I've spawned throughout the eons," he attempted to clarify the situation.

"Hel's mother, an immortal giant, was banished for eternity to Helheim by Odin because he was afraid of the daughter she was about to bear. For me to have a child with a human... with *you*... terrifies them all."

"But why, Loki? I don't understand," Sela wailed brokenly.

There were no words in all the languages of Earth or the tongues of Old Norse which could convince Sela their child had to die *at all*, never mind before it had the chance to draw its first breath?

This was contemptible.

Sela rested a hand on her belly, feeling a responding kick. No freaking way were they going to harm her child. She would give her life to ensure its survival, painfully aware her life was another thing they would take without compunction.

"I'll explain later. Right now, it is imperative you gather what we need to get out of here. It's only a matter of time before this place is over-run by Norse deities and I'd just as soon not be here when they arrive."

Sela punched Loki in the chest for dodging the question.

This damn god is too skilled at obfuscation.

While acknowledging she was not going to get any more information out of him until he was good and ready, Sela gave him a pleading look, hoping to penetrate his implacable façade.

"Nice try, but no." Loki kissed her soundly.

Sela controlled her frustration, and slid off his lap.

She opened their *neatly organized* closet cautiously. She had been pestering Loki to add extra shelving since they moved in; something he had promised 'to get to next weekend.'

Looks like you won't have to bother now.

Sela dug out their emergency pack, glad Loki had insisted they have one, his reasoning unclear until this moment.

Propping it against the doorjamb, she reached up to the shelf above, to grab a long sleeved, blue and white striped T, and her bib overalls — the cute, faded denim ones with the strategically placed rips.

She had bought a larger size than she needed, specifically to wear during her pregnancy. Wriggling into them, Sela discovered they still fitted, if a tad snugly.

Folding the bottom cuffs, she pulled on a pair of socks and slid her feet into her Doc Martens.

Rifling on the same shelf, she found her favorite sweatshirt and tugged it on. Sela had no idea what Notre Dame meant, but she liked the logo. It had been free anyway, a requisition from the church's donation bin.

Sela studied her reflection critically.

Fortunately, in this city, no one questioned people's fashion choices; she could strut through Times Square in a skimpy bikini or a suit of chain mail and no one would notice. Overalls and DM's under a black trench coat wouldn't raise an eyebrow.

You gotta love New York.

She definitely rocked this look — pregnant or not. Running her fingers through her flaming red hair, she swept it up into a scruffy bun.

Sela smirked impishly. *Eat your heart out, Freya.*

Shouldering the pack, her next stop was the weapons cabinet.

The glitter of her blades greeted her when she yanked the doors wide. As she did every time she saw them, Sela was held motionless by their magnificence, but she had no time to loiter, and admiration ebbed as she sheathed the pair.

Next, she retrieved the pistol Loki had gifted her, so thoughtfully, on that snowy night when she found herself *naked* in Central Park.

She had yet to forgive him for that little oversight.

Sela slid the gun into its holster, which she strapped over her shoulder.

The weapon might prove useless against what we are about to face but, considering where it came from, it couldn't hurt.

As Sela checked to see whether there was anything else worth taking, she noticed Loki's blade was absent.

These people are supposed to be his family, yet it was obvious he felt it necessary to go armed, Sela shook her head at the notion.

She turned to Loki, whose breath lodged in his throat at the beauty of his woman, dressed for battle.

I would die for her.

He wished he had the courage to tell her, but feared she would not believe his avowal.

Rising from the bed, and crossing the room, he whisked her into his arms, hoping this was enough to tell her what was in his heart.

Their lips met in a passionate kiss, one that lasted all too briefly.

Sela broke away, saying, "Time for that later, *ástin mín*, we have much to do."

Taking his hand, she led him to the apartment door. Stopping long enough for Loki to collect his sword from where he had propped it earlier.

Without another word, the two went into the night... unsure of their next move.

TWO

It was centuries since Freya had found herself not only in Valhalla, but also before Odin's throne.

Even though here of her own volition, Freya felt like the prodigal child awaiting retribution for past sins. She refused to allow this to reflect in her demeanor; her expression, one of long-suffering boredom.

It was imperative she looked confident or her ruse would fail, relieved Odin was unaware that Myst's ability to tap into or corrupt the powers of the other inhabitants of Valhalla, did not extend to her.

She almost burst out laughing when the self-righteous blowhard sniped, "Look what the cats dragged in."

Freya added silently, *literally*.

"To what do I owe the honor of your presence, wife?"

Feigning surprise, Freya gushed, "Oh my beloved husband, you remembered we are joined? My heart surely skips a beat at your generous acknowledgment. Might I inquire whether you pined for me or wondered where my absence took me?" she asked, her sarcasm withering.

She tapped her chin with her index finger as though

pondering the validity of her question. "Doubtful, too busy being distracted by your various concubines—"

"Concubines?" Odin blustered, his fingers curled around the arms of his throne, his knuckles whitening with the pressure.

His face twisted into a scowl as he straightened his posture. "You should watch your silver-tipped tongue, wife. You were once numbered among them."

Freya smiled inwardly. The only way to make this sound genuine was for her to fire it up as a certain rancher would say. Her chest pinching in recollection.

She baited the hook.

"No, Odin. All I ever represented to you was a means to consolidate your status among the realms, and I was naught but a naive girl who yearned to believe your empty promises.

"I prevailed, despite your careless destruction of my heart but, as a result, your callous indifference no longer touches me. I have nothing left for you... or anybody else..." a claim she knew was a bald-faced lie "...to harm."

Odin scoffed. After an eon together, regardless that it was millennia ago, he believed he knew this woman better than anyone.

"I'm sure your dear friend Loki has touched you more than a few times... along with any number of mortals... so do not try to play the victim. It is unbecoming for one of your stature, Freya."

From the table by his elbow, Odin retrieved a horn of mead and guzzled it to ease his anger, determined not to let her distract his attention.

It is my responsibility to control the realms and all who reside in them, not this annoying bitch's, he reminded himself, using his cuff to swipe the remnants of the mead's foam from his beard.

In an effort to regain the upper hand, he adopted a more diplomatic tone. "So what brings you back to my hallowed halls? To beg forgiveness for your adulterous antics?"

Freya did not bother to stifle her condescending laugh. "Are you serious, you cantankerous old lech? I come to request a formal dissolution of this debacle of a union. I am wearied of watching you make a mockery of our marriage."

"You chase that scoundrel from one end of Yggdrasil to the other, even try to wed some feckless mortal behind my back, and now you have the effrontery to petition for a — what do the Midgardian's call it? — ah yes, a divorce. Do you think he is more capable than I of bringing you happiness?"

Skirting passed the feckless mortal reference, Freya rebutted, "Are you blind? Do you not know Loki has claimed a mate and, as much as I hate to admit it, one of whom he might be worthy?"

Steeling herself, Freya summoned up all her guile and, with apparent frustration, blurted out, "While I waste my breath on you... she carries his..."

Deliberately, she broke off mid-sentence and assumed a horrified expression, as though her revelation was unintentional.

She held her breath... this *had* to work....

Odin's face darkened to a shade of red reserved for boiled lobsters, clearly visible despite his thick white beard.

"The human is pregnant with his child?"

Is she saying the Fates have plotted against me to ensure prophecy will come to fruition?

"N-No, Odin, y-your failing ears misheard. I was about to say, she carries his s-sword. He has taught her to fight like a god." Behaving with uncharacteristic agitation, Freya instilled a note of distress into her repudiation.

"Freya, do you think me addled? I watched her grow from childhood. Her skills predate Loki's interference."

Leaning back in his throne, Odin stroked his beard, ruminating over this galling snippet.

If Freya's prattle is true, I will not have much time to rid myself of this burgeoning bane.

"Do not lie to me, wife. When is the child due?"

"I-I cannot be certain, Odin." Freya simpered, thankful Myst could not read her mind.

"Bah. Your ignorance matters not. I have trustworthy vassals to do my bidding and unearth the truth."

Rising, he circled his wife, stalking to the banqueting table where he refilled his horn.

After a long swallow, quenching his desire to smite Freya, he said, without turning, "If you wish to rid yourself of me... although for the life of me, I cannot conceive why... you must earn it."

Freya felt a trickle of foreboding. While this was the reaction she had hoped for, a bargain with Odin was never to the advantage of the one to whom he proposed it. Pompous jerk.

"I'm listening," she forced herself to sound resigned.

Setting down his horn, Odin did not move, his back a rigid barrier.

The tension in the air thickened as the silence stretched out.

Freya was on the verge of giving vent to an ear-splitting scream when Odin, a smile painted on his face, pivoted slowly.

His voice softened as he lied through his teeth, "I wish to contact the happy couple, to bid them every happiness on their nuptials... despite my dismay at not being invited." He allowed a hint of sadness to wash over his features for added effect.

Despite the breakdown of her friendship with Sela, Freya was not childish... or cruel enough to deliver this spiteful god to Sela and Loki's doorstep.

"I have not seen them since my... extended holiday," she prevaricated.

The harsh laughter grated on her ears. "Ah yes, your temporary aberration with the Irish whelp. A situation resolved satisfactorily... if belatedly." He leered unattractively.

"Who you bed matters not. We all have itches which require scratching, as long as you adhere to the rules, but debauching yourself to those lesser beings has contaminated you, leaving you undesirable."

"And your reason before that?" Freya chastised with a sardonic curl of her lip, relieved he did not appear to be aware of her most recent... liaison.

Odin ignored the jibe. "I should rid you of the temptations of your toys on Midgard all together." He waved a dismissive hand. "A task for another day.

"Since you were the last of us to see Loki, I want you to deliver an invitation to attend a ceremony in his honor here in the Hall."

"Does that include his woman as well?"

"Absolutely not," Odin's reply boomed like a crack of thunder.

He heaved a calming breath. "Sela has yet to prove herself worthy of admittance. The rumors of her life and punishment are legendary."

He chuckled. "Let's call it a belated bachelor party. I believe that is the term mortals use."

By all the Gods, the plan is working. Stunned, for she did not expect him to fall so neatly or so quickly, into her trap, Freya strove to remain impassive.

Of course it is, a voice in her head tutted. *We almost have him... do not lose focus.*

The voice was correct, Odin was definitely up to something, but there was more than the obvious at stake here, most especially, the two whom she was determined to protect from his wrath. They were more important than worrying about the Asgardian's motives, however reprehensible.

Freya managed to quirk a suspicious brow. Odin's reason was not yet subsumed by his delusions. She needed to maintain the deception... just a little longer.

"I shall pass on your invitation, on the proviso you do not renege on your word."

"I would never think of it, dear Freya... as long as you keep me abreast of anything you learn. No matter how minute."

"That's all you want?"

"Upon my honor."

"We both know how worthless that is, but you leave me no choice."

Freya's haste to beat a judicious retreat from her future ex-husband, was halted at the door by a sly question.

"Tell me, how do you intend to manage on your own?

We both know you do not have the competence to survive without magic, at least, not without bringing unwanted attention to yourself. You will crawl back to my feet before long."

"Do not hold your breath."

Making a show of storming from the Hall, Freya climbed into her carriage and was swept away by her faithful cats.

Reaching a safe distance from Odin, Freya said aloud, "Okay, girl, that part has been taken care of. Now what?"

You will find your car in a parking garage outside the city.

"The keys?" Freya countered to her unseen accomplice.

Keys? What are keys? All you asked me to do was put your stupid car somewhere you could find it.

Freya huffed. "Fine, I'll figure something out. Now, is there any chance you are going to tell me what this is all about?"

THREE

Since ridding the world of Peer, Sela had not rested on her laurels.

She had missed out on too much during the last millennium to allow that to happen and, consequently, ensured she did everything in her power to expand her knowledge of... well... everything.

She had immersed herself in the 115th Street Library for hours, reading whatever she could get her hands on concerning history.

The New York museums had grown so accustomed to her presence, she had been invited to conduct more than a few tours owing to her uncanny knowledge of Norse history and mythology.

If only they had only known she could introduce them to a live *myth* and change their stale exhibit to an interactive one. Unfortunately, that required an act of faith which, Sela discovered, these people had long since abandoned.

Another source of twenty-first century education — and welcome distraction from day-to day life — was the very instrument of their escape from the city.

The sleek, black 1940 Ford coupe, which Loki had surprised her with on the first anniversary of the night he asked her to spend eternity with him, awaited them.

At the time, she had teased him saying with a cheeky wink, "If this a bribe so I won't leave your side, it *definitely* swings the vote in your favor."

Even though the car had come into her life as a rusted heap, and only ran on six of the eight cylinders, she loved it *almost* as much as she loved her husband.

After adding a few... okay, a lot more... dents while learning to drive, she set about restoring it.

Thanks once more to the public library system, she modified the coupe as far as humanly possible without the car losing its originality.

Sela had joked that if she could not fix Loki, at least she could fix his gift.

She glanced across at the hulking figure, illuminated by the moon and the soft glow of the dash.

Sela regretted her bout of temper, keenly aware he was only trying to protect her, which exacerbated her hatred for everyone who had attended the meeting and who now sought to destroy their child.

She would see them pay for their complicity.

Sela drove through the night, reminded of the story of another couple, Mani and Sol, hounded in a never-ending pursuit by the Norse deities.

According to the legends, the duo were brother and sister, in charge of the sun and moon. Like her own beloved, their origins were steeped in mystery, and the extent of their powers not revealed until the time was right.

Once the gods became aware, two massive wolves, Skol and Hati, were sent to hunt them down.

Why the gods would set in motion an event like this, Sela could never understand. *If the wolves ever caught up with Mani and Sol, would it not mean the end of all creation?*

Then again, very few things the gods did, made sense. Their entire existence seemed based on the premise of destroying each other.

Is not the fact, I'm behind the wheel, fleeing from a city I love, in order to save my child's life, proof?

Maybe it was too much inbreeding, or cross breeding, or simply self-loathing.

Just thinking about the reasons gave Sela a headache.

A riddle best left unsolved.

Checking the gas gauge, Sela noticed the pointer hovering on *Empty*. For once it was a relief rather than a nuisance to own an ancient gas-guzzler. She was ready for a break.

Exiting the Interstate, she was pleased to see the lights of an all-night truck stop. Pulling up to the pumps, she began her usual ritual.

Digging through her bag, Sela cursed the evil demons who invented those damnable credit cards. To this day, she accused Peer of the deed.

It was one thing when a person could use bits of gold and silver to purchase what they needed, the concept of invisible money placed on a piece of plastic, which she was forever losing, was a whole other matter... and one Sela had yet to grasp.

Employing her most honeyed tone, she woke her husband, "Ást?"

Sela waited for a grumpy eye to peek open, followed by Loki's lecture on adult responsibility once he discerned what she required. Considering the source, it always made her laugh. The god of childish pranks attempting to set her straight.

This time, there was no scolding look and no stern voice, just the appearance of her credit card from his pocket, and silence.

Yet another incentive to hate this loathsome situation.

Whipping the card from his fingers, Sela alighted, and shoved the cursed plastic into the pump. Chilly fingers fumbled with the nozzle, but she managed to insert it, and started to fill her car.

The cold night wind swirled about her.

Out of habit, she studied the collection of travelers performing the same mundane task. She envied them because they were going somewhere safe and warm.

She, on the other hand, was on a reckless drive to the north, not even sure why they were going in that direction.

The task complete, Sela was about to return the nozzle to the pump when something stopped her. The wind died down, and a strange foreboding crept up her spine. She spun around.

At first, she failed to see anything except the cold night. It was not until the lights of a passing car flickered across an icy body, that the creature came into focus.

"Take this, Niflheim," Sela's voice held an ominous note.

She sprayed gallons of gas on the ice creature, narrowly missing being slashed by its heavy blade. She made sure it was drenched before it could attack again.

Sela heard it scream when realization dawned. A

wicked smile curled her lips, and she pulled her lighter from her pocket, flicking it into life.

"Let Odin know there will be hell to pay for threatening a pregnant woman," she warned, and pitched the lighter at the ice creature who attempted to flee.

She took great joy in watching it explode into a shower of ice shards. Its enchanted body extinguished the flames before they could spread or draw anyone else's attention.

With a triumphant flourish, Sela replaced the nozzle in its cradle, and slammed the cap, twisting it until she heard the lock click.

"Fuck with me, will they?" she sneered, and turned to head inside for food, walking smack bang into Loki.

He looked from the pool of water to her.

There were a litany of reasons why her reaction to the intruder was imprudent, but he didn't bother explaining; they would fall on deaf ears.

Besides, now they had bigger problems.

They had been found too quickly and not even Loki had expected that. It would only be a matter of time before something else appeared.

Hooking his arm through hers, he escorted her into the truck stop.

Sela had expected a congratulatory *well done* from her husband, but he remained taciturn as he ushered her through the doors.

Fed up with the silent treatment, she growled, "You know, I'm more than capable of buying food myself."

"Wanted to make sure you didn't forget the jerky like you usually do," Loki countered mildly.

"You know that stuff will kill you." Sela actually pouted.

They both laughed softly at that. With everything Sela

did for him, knowing how and when to make him laugh, pleased Loki almost as much as her fire in bed.

He let Sela wander off to forage for what passed as food nowadays. Loki missed the challenge of hunting wild game or fishing in the fjords but, like Sela, he had no alternative but to learn the new ways, to adapt to the modern world they now inhabited.

Loki picked one of the magazines from the rack chronicling the latest in hunting equipment, modeled by scantily clad women in camouflage gear.

"Only game getting mounted is her." He smiled, flipping through the pages.

Rather than reading the magazine he was leafing through, Loki used it as a way to study the forecourt covertly.

Any one of those travelers could be another assassin, he thought. He maintained a close vigil on the coupe, ensuring no one made a move towards it.

"How long do you think we have before the next one pops up?" Loki sensed Sela beside him even before she spoke.

Loki drew in an apprehensive breath, an unconscious trait but one which annoyed Sela, because it made him sound like a drama queen.

"I'm not sure." He exhaled. "I'm still trying to figure out how the Niflheimian located us so easily, but no doubt the valkyries are aware and have passed the word onto Odin. I suggest we hurry up and get off the main road."

Sela added a map to her collection of odds and ends for their crazy road trip. Her GPS was not functioning properly out here, and the map might give her some idea where Loki was taking them.

She wanted to ask him but, inexplicably, feared the answer.

As the pair climbed into the coupe, she slipped a piece of red licorice between her teeth like a cigar.

Sela likened herself to a captain of a bomber taking off for war. Passing the map to her husband, she commanded, "Ok, Navigator, plot the course."

Loki rolled his eyes at her and chuckled. "Aye, Cap'n. Take a right, and keep driving until I tell you when to turn."

"So, you're gonna leave me flying blind, are you?" Sela canted her head. A swift kick from a tiny foot curbed her tongue.

Even their child was trying to tell her it was a waste of time asking.

Huffing peevishly, Sela pointed the heavy car at the pitch-black road. Glancing in the rearview mirror as they drove away, Sela wanted to make sure they were alone.

Once the glow from the truck stop vanished, she paid more heed to the emptiness in front, and less on the mirror.

She failed to notice the flicker of lights following them at a discreet distance.

FOUR

The usual raucous revelry of Valhalla was nowhere to be found this eve. Any which may have lingered in the hall, was drowned out by the pounding of Odin's boots as he stormed across the floor, and the echo of his curses as he bellowed for answers.

"Who gave the command for the foolish chunk of ice to attack her?" Odin roared. ***"Its only mission was to follow them and keep me informed as to their whereabouts."***

Odin paused to wash the taste of failure from his mouth. A loss was acceptable in battle, but a loss because of stupidity was unforgivable.

He flung the empty horn aside, like a petulant brat having a tantrum, watching it splinter when it hit the wall.

Inhaling slowly in an attempt to collect himself, Odin knew his vehement tirade meant no one in their right minds would be willing to admit responsibility.

Craven cowards.

*It is imperative, they understand my orders are the **only** ones to be followed, and any actions without my approval shall not be tolerated.*

"Now, thanks to that moron, not only do they know we were close enough to end this, but also that nonsense resulted in them disappearing from the face of that cursed pile of spinning rock. Can nobody in this *fucking* Hall heed a simple command?"

Odin detested human obscenities because they came from an inferior realm. Resorting to one, made him feel deficient and unable to control the situation.

Tonight, however, he gaged the vulgar term justified. It was the only way to make the imbeciles surrounding him appreciate his anger.

Finally, Hodor, the God of Winter, risked confessing, "Mighty Odin, it was I who unleashed the ice creature upon the pair. The moment was at hand and Loki knew we were—"

"**Silence**," Odin's voice shook the walls. "When your worthless hide comes to rule this Hall, then and only then, shall you be allowed to execute decisions without my approval."

Without warning or thought, Odin drew his mighty blade from its sheath and cleaved Hodor in two.

Blood cascaded from each half, staining the thick oak flooring, pooling between the slats to trickle out like a spider's web, and the coppery tang of Hodor's lifeforce permeated the Hall.

Odin muttered under his breath, "Didn't want the burden of leadership to weigh you down, Hodor. Enjoy your time with that bitch, Hel."

Turning to those remaining in the room, Odin flicked the crimson drenched blade, purposely splattering Hodor's blood in their direction in gruesome emphasis.

"Should any of you wish to join your brother in the pits of Helheim, speak up now and I will be happy to oblige.

Otherwise, every action must be cleared by me. Insubordination will not be tolerated. Is that understood?"

Odin's icy tone was more terrifying than his ire.

The assemblage hurried to acknowledge Odin's edict while trying, in vain, *not* to gawk at the remains of Hodor.

Odin summoned the valkyries and commanded them to remove the mutilated corpse.

Preferring not to watch, Odin walked to the massive table to retrieve another horn of ale. Alcohol seemed to be the only elixir mighty enough to quell his anger this evening.

As they set about their task, the youngest of the valkyries, Svipul, froze in terror when she recognized the body.

She had spent more than a few nights warming the God of Winter's bed, eventually becoming his confidante.

Discovering what he had done, she had pleaded with him not to admit responsibility in fear of Odin's wrath. Hodor's honesty and pride would not allow him to hide in silence.

Reconciling herself to the loss of her lover because he had dared to act independently of Odin's insanity was bad enough, to have to wash away his remains was more than Svipul could bear.

Devastated, she tried to steel her emotions muttering wrathfully, "The severity of this punishment is intolerable. I swear, my beloved Hodor, your death will not go unavenged."

She would make sure the crazy old god could no longer mete out death on a whim. Leveling her brilliant blue eyes at the Asgardian's back, Svipul reached for her dagger, intent on burying the blade into Odin's murderous flesh.

Her intent thwarted by a hand gripping her wrist.

Svipul pivoted on her heel ready to channel her fury on whoever dared interfere, to see Herja — her twin and older by the twinkling of an eye — wrestling to prevent her from making an irreparable mistake.

In the calmest and softest voice she could summon, Herja murmured, "No, Svi, tonight is not the time."

Svipul's eyes slid away from her sister's tender gaze, turning cold and deadly as they zeroed on Odin's back.

In undertones, Herja consoled, "Never fear, Svi, we will use your powers of Fate to destroy him at the opportune moment. For now, we will take your love, and honor his death."

Odin studied the valkyries as they vanished with Hodor's body, acutely aware of the uneasiness hanging like a pall over the room. He shrugged it off. A problem for another time.

With his attention otherwise engaged, the majority of the Norse Deities deemed it wise to vanish.

Only Odin's son, Baldr, opted to tarry, lifting his gaze from the stained floor where the mighty and faithful Hodor had stood, to his father.

"Was that necessary?" His question dripped with disdain for Odin's reckless and infantile action.

"One day you will understand, my son, that respect, loyalty, and dedication can only be sustained by force and through fear. If you allow others to usurp your jurisdiction, they will soon find little need for your existence. So yes, Hodor got what he deserved."

Baldr shook his head and turned to leave the Great Hall,

disillusioned both by Odin's ridiculous philosophy and the old man himself.

Odin allowed him to reach the door before he spoke, "Baldr."

Baldr paused, clutching the ornate handle, wanting nothing more than to be on the other side of the door and away from his father.

Unconsciously, Baldr mocked Odin by mimicking a cue he had picked up by observing his father throughout the ages. When the elder was obliged to endure a conversation, he wanted no part of, he blew the same jaded sigh Baldr now heaved.

"Yes, Father?"

"Do you understand why we cannot allow anyone to act on their own accord?"

Oddly, Odin's tone suggested he was seeking a stamp of approval from his offspring.

"Because you said so," Baldr retorted, and stormed out.

The last words he heard were a flurry of obscenities, followed by a bawled demand for Freya to appear before him.

Baldr knew his command would fall on deaf ears. His mother was elsewhere, carrying out her own plans.

FIVE

Had Loki informed Sela, up front, their destination was Canada, she would have stayed on Interstate 87 and arrived in time for a late breakfast.

Instead, she was obliged to follow Loki's convoluted route along the back roads, doubling the length of their journey.

By the middle of the dreary afternoon, they were still on America soil, and, if Sela was not mistaken, about to be battered by a late season blizzard.

Weary from concentrating on the winding roads, Sela had demanded they stop, and the couple was currently ensconced in a seedy dive in Plattsburgh, New York arguing over their chances of crossing the border.

"The passports were in the weapons cabinet where they always are. What possessed you to leave them there?" Loki fumed, trying not to make a scene, with limited success, it must be admitted. "This is just like you, woman, always going off half-cocked."

"Well, dumbass, if you had taken two seconds to tell me we needed them, perhaps we wouldn't be in this mess, but nooooo, you have to keep everything a damn secret until we're stuck in this damn border town with no damn way across. Is this where I say, 'Yay...great plan'?"

Angrily, Sela swiped her last french-fry through the dollop of ketchup, and shoved it in her mouth. Fighting with Loki wouldn't solve anything, but she was tired of being kept in the dark.

Loki studied his wife.

Beyond a shadow of a doubt, despite all the women he had bedded in the eons he had been in the realms, Sela was the only one to own his heart — something to which even Freya could not lay claim.

He deplored causing her stress, but had no choice. Looping his arm around her, he said quietly, "We're aiming for Newfoundland."

Sela was caught off guard. "Excuse me? We're going *where*?"

"You heard me, Newfoundland."

"Why on earth are we going there? Did you get some sort of hotel deal on the computer? Maybe a spa resort weekend?"

Sela assumed there was a specific reason for their head-long dash to the edge of civilization and felt she had the right to know what it was.

Snatching a fry from Loki's plate, Sela threw caution to the winds and decided to extract as much truth as humanly possible from her husband.

"So, tell me, Oh God of the Impossible, how in the name of your Damnable Daughter are we supposed to get to Bum Fuck Egypt?"

Sela was proud of her knowledge of twenty-first century slang, even if she didn't always use it in the right context.

"Is damn your word of the day?" Loki countered, "And kindly leave Hel out of this, for if she is involved at all, I'm certain, for the moment, she's on the sidelines. As for getting to where we need to go, I thought we could charter a flight out of Montreal—"

"You want me to ditch my car in some airport parking lot? Are you insane? There's a better chance I'll leave your ass there." Sela exploded, forgetting where they were.

The quarreling couple brought the restaurant to an awkward pause and, for a moment, became the object of every other patron's scrutiny.

Sela's, "**What?**" accompanied by her evil eye was deterrent enough to anyone who presumed to interfere.

Even the pretty young waitress who had dared to flirt with Loki, approached the table with a healthy degree of caution, to ask Sela whether they needed anything else.

"Thank you, no," Sela smiled sweetly, and waved her away, scouring the Canadian atlas to find a suitable way to traverse Canada without surrendering her precious car.

Fortunately, she discovered the Trans-Canada Highway.

Spinning the atlas around, so her husband could see, Sela jabbed her finger on the page, "There, see, we *can* drive across," she said in defense of her car.

"You do realize it will take at least two or three days, if we get there at all." An exasperated Loki huffed. "If we fly, we can be there tonight."

"Nope," Sela emphasized the *p*. "We're gonna drive. Besides, I hate flying."

Her breezy smile did not fool Loki, acutely aware how fearful she was at the notion of being crammed into a metal tube with wings. Facing the army of valkyries, led by Odin himself, was less terrifying.

He brought Sela's hand to his lips and kissed her palm gently, hiding a knowing smirk. As fearless as his wife appeared, it was still amusing to see the vulnerability of her humanity peek through.

One day she might remember her new immortality, Loki mused to himself.

He relinquished his grasp and rose from the table. Sela cocked a brow, trying to work out what he was up to.

"Greasy lunch not sitting well in your delicate belly? I'm sure I have something for that in my bag."

Sela knew full well, Loki could eat anything he wanted. In fact, she had been honored to witness him devour an entire moose, horns and all, in a single sitting.

"Not quite, my love, but even gods have to answer the call of nature. And I'm sure you don't want me to pollute the car."

"You do and I'll filet you like a trout. It took me weeks to fumigate it, the last time you couldn't control your..." she smiled and said with exaggerated politeness, "...flatulence."

Loki could not help his rumble of laughter because the car was basically unusable until it had aired out. Never again would Sela persuade him to eat asparagus.

"Check the maps while you're waiting, hon. We need to get over the border and I would like to do so before we have to suffer another course of this fine cuisine," Loki implored as he vanished from the table.

Sela scrutinized the atlas, absent-mindedly finishing the rest of Loki's fries.

Time slipped by until that all too familiar foot in her belly gave her a boot, demanding she pay attention.

She was going to miss the extra intuition gained while carrying their child — although the foot she would be happy to do without.

Glancing up from her maps, she noticed the rest of the restaurant had emptied and an older waitress was standing next to her. The woman seemed to be studying the routes almost as intently as Sela.

"You and the hubby on vacation?" The waitress's attempt at civil conversation sounded scripted, the typical mundane small-talk doled out to every customer, but Sela welcomed a chance to talk about anything except their impending doom.

"Not so much a vacation, as a business trip," Sela replied genially, knowing the woman could not possibly understand what they were going through.

How could she?

Sela had no clue as to why any of this was happening or why it was vital, they reach Newfoundland.

"Kind of a strange time of the year for a road trip don't ya think? Must be important if you're being dragged across the continent in your shape," the waitress contended as she topped up Sela's coffee.

Sela was warned about the possible repercussions of drinking too much coffee during her pregnancy, but some habits were hard to break.

"Especially, if your husband is taking you to that God forsaken plot of dirt," the waitress seemed compelled to add. "You two archeologists? Only reason I could think, as to why you'd want to drive all the way out there."

Already annoyed, Sela was unsettled by the waitress's leading questions.

She shut the atlas with a snap, and gathered her things.

Her eyes slid to the door, willing Loki to get back here right now, while the waitress droned on about the dangers of a pregnant woman traveling.

Instinct prompted Sela to take a closer look at the woman's eyes. Something about them sent a chill through Sela and fear prickled her nape.

Desperately, she behaved as though naught was amiss. "I'll be careful. If I could get my check, we'll be on our way," she chirped cheerily.

The older woman shrugged, totaled up the bill, tore it from the pad and handed it to Sela whose fingers curled around the paper, as the bell above the door chimed. Her gaze swung to the hulking figure filling the door frame.

It was Loki. Sela exhaled a sigh of relief.

Digging in her pocket, she withdrew a wad of cash to settle her account, but when she turned to give the nosy busybody a piece of her mind in lieu of a tip, the waitress was not the same woman.

Sela was surprised to see the girl who had served them.

"T-that will be $17.50, ma'am," she said in subdued tones, unwilling to call the ire of this crazy woman down on her head.

Silently, Sela peeled off a twenty without taking her eyes off the girl. The poor waitress snatched the money and scurried away before Sela could tell her to keep the change.

Loki pressed himself against Sela, whispering into her ear, "Please don't tell me you threatened her life just because she found your husband charming and irresistible."

Sela replied flatly, "Don't start, and unless you have figured out a way to get us over the border, you'd do well not to speak."

Loki dropped two passports on the table before scooping Sela's stack of maps.

Sela picked both up and leafed through them, disconcerted when the contents seemed to flicker.

"Hopefully the border guards won't study them too assiduously. With all the shit that's going on, it's hard to concentrate which affects my magic. Transforming the tourist maps didn't take as well as I hoped, but they should bear up to brief scrutiny," Loki tried to reassure.

Sela didn't care, all she wanted was to be anywhere but here.

Handing them back to Loki, something else on the table caught her eye.

It was the receipt.

Why would the waitress leave a second one?

The mysterious scrap of paper baffled Sela because she swore the original was in her hand, curiosity impelling her to check her clenched fist.

Controlling the urge, she asked Loki to take the stuff to the car while she freshened up.

Her husband smiled and did as his wife bade, strolling out to the car, maps in hand.

With Loki temporarily occupied, Sela unfurled her fingers to see nothing but thin air.

Her eyes widened as her gaze swung to the pristine receipt begging to be read. Nerveless fingers lifting it from the scuffed tabletop.

On the face of the receipt, in overly dramatic cursive flair, a detailed itemization of their order.

But Sela could see something written on the back. Flipping it over, she was greeted with a message scrawled in ancient Norse.

Dauðinn
fylgir þér og
svo geri ég
það

Death follows you, and so do I.

SIX

This time, Sela was happier *not* to be on the interstate. The decision to take Route 22 north meant they would bypass the major Customs Service Station, and only have to contend with a smaller regional one.

By the time they reached the crossing, the sun had set and the predicted snowstorm was lashing the area.

What they expected to be an easy pass into Canada, turned into a song and dance the exhausted travelers had not foreseen.

A surly border agent, pissed at having to abandon the warmth of his cozy office took his sweet time deciding whether he should let them through.

Loki's magic lasted until the agent returned their 'passports and accompanying identification,' at which point, they reverted to bright glossy pictures of Niagara Falls in its unadulterated splendor.

Fortunately, the father of five was too busy lecturing Sela about the dangers of traveling so late in her pregnancy to notice. She smiled and let him prattle on, thinking how relieved she would be when the baby was born, and she no longer had to endure the oft repeated sermon.

When it came to the 'documentation' detailing the weapons they were transporting into Canada and why, the official quirked a brow as he read them. Listening to the lame explanation from the suspicious couple, in the souped-up coupe, he considered running them in.

"Damn Americans," he muttered under his breath. "They don't look like terrorists... but they ain't armed for hunting bear, either."

Swinging the beam of his flashlight from the back of the car to Sela's face, he contemplated whether it was worth his time and the extra paperwork their arrest would necessitate.

The dark interior helped conceal the beads of sweat dripping from Loki's forehead as he gave up on the conceal-ment spell. Slumping into his seat, fatigued and irritated by the confrontation, he directed the last of his concentration on the agent.

Silently, Loki advised the man to let them through or become dinner. A strange look descended on the border agent's features and, abruptly, he changed his tune.

"Your husband's not looking too well, ma'am. There's some decent motels just outside Montreal, where I'd recommend stopping for the night, especially in your condition. I wouldn't want you getting stuck in this storm."

Sela fired up the coupe and put the car in gear.

"Thanks officer, we'll be sure to take you up on your famous Canadian hospitality. Stay warm," she trilled, with a wide smile, as she drove away, carefully, ignoring the temptation to gun the engine.

The instant the crossing was out of sight, she shot Loki an anxious glance.

Sela had never seen her husband look so pale and drawn after what should have been a simple parlor trick. She wanted to get him somewhere safe to rest — sleep would be a welcome gift for both of them.

The snow was accumulating rapidly as they traveled north to Montreal. Valiantly, snow ploughs strove to prevent it from banking up, but it was a losing battle. Sela had to slow down to keep the car on the snow-packed road delaying their arrival further.

With Loki succumbing to exhaustion, Sela decided the weather had won this duel, and turned into the first motel parking lot they came across. She frowned at the number of similarly stranded travelers hoping to find shelter for the night.

The couple were lucky to get one of the last rooms available.

The over-inflated price led Sela to quip, as she snatched the key from the receptionist's hand, "And they call my ancestors marauders. I'm just glad you have Wi-Fi."

"Next motel is ten miles down the road, if you don't want the room, I'll wager anyone in that queue will pay twice as much for it. As for the net, I wouldn't count on the connection staying up. Have a good night."

The sounds of irritated guests complaining about the price and quality of the place thrummed through the paper-thin walls as Sela and Loki trudged to their room.

The pair had learned, eons ago, that any cave in a storm was shelter, and right now, a cave would be better than this dump.

No sooner had Sela opened the door, than Loki edged past her to collapse on the bed.

Before she had got one foot inside, she knew Loki was fast asleep by the sound of his snores, which, to anyone else, could be mistaken for the mating call of a moose.

Aware she wasn't going to get any sleep in the foreseeable future, Sela curled up on the loveseat and switched on the television.

Flicking through the channels, she settled on the local news. Pictures of cars littering the motorway kicked off the evening report while the newscaster pleaded with motorists to stay off the road.

One vehicle in particular prompted Sela to frown in disgust — a classic blue and black Mercury Cougar stuck nose first in a snowdrift.

"What friggin' idiot would be driving a beautiful car like that in this storm?" Sela groused to herself. By the time they reached the weather report, she had given up hope of hearing any positive news.

The weatherman *did* manage to bolster her mood slightly when he *almost* guaranteed the blizzard would end by morning. On that cheerful note, Sela flicked off the television and decided to join her husband.

A discarded trail of clothes behind her, Sela stood next to the bed.

Her holstered gun still slung over her shoulder, she ran her eyes along Loki's slumbering body.

It occurred to her that, lately, their frequent and torrid lovemaking had dwindled to zero, in part due to Loki's concern that having sex would harm the baby... despite Sela's assurance to the contrary. The sight of her drop-dead gorgeous hunk of a man lying splayed across the bed stirred a desire within Sela which needed slaking.

Flinging her holster over the bedpost, she kneeled on

the covers, teasing open the buttons of Loki's shirt to expose his taut abs.

She scattered kisses across his chest, smiling to herself when she heard a deep rumble, followed by fingers snarling through her hair.

"Are you sure it's safe?" he growled in her ear.

"You can't get me any more pregnant." A gurgle of mirth slid over her lips.

"I mean, will it harm the babe?"

Sela stretched sinuously, hearing Loki catch his breath. "I keep telling you, the books say it's fine."

"Well, we can't argue with the books." Loki grinned wickedly, his hands roaming over her willowy body, playing her like a virtuoso musician.

Infinitesimal waves of pleasure started to glissade along Sela's spine as their lips met in a searing kiss.

For the next little while, consumed by their fiery passion, the fear lurking around them faded into insignificance.

Satiated and content, Sela pressed a light kiss to her husband's chest and curled into the crook of his massive arm, listening to the drum of his heart.

After a few moments, and although unwilling to spoil the mood, she ventured, "Feeling better? I've never seen you struggle with magic like that—"

Loki stopped Sela mid-sentence, propping her on his chest, his fingers chasing errant strands of hair from her face and did his best to reassure.

"I'm fine, *ástin mín*. It's just been difficult to stay focused. I vow to keep you out of harm's way and give you my word there will be no more unstable magic."

He kissed her tenderly, then tucked her back into the safety of his arm.

Sela nestled there quietly, waiting for him to doze off.

The sex had worked wonders for her and she hoped it had done the same for Loki. A sigh of relief escaped her when she heard the customary moose call signaling oblivion had reclaimed him.

Slowly, Sela joined him.

The darkness which greeted her was the antithesis of a pleasant dream.

Confronting her, Loki's overly-protective daughter, Hel — her face twisted and brooding, her huge arms folded, apparently affronted that she had been kept waiting.

The hatred between the two was palpable, and Sela was thankful Loki had taught her one of his most important tricks — materializing anything she wished into her dreams.

He had warned her about being unprepared for battle, and this seemed the perfect time to heed his advice.

Resting her hands on the pommels of her trusted swords as they appeared by her sides, Sela met the infuriated gaze of the giantess.

The silence lengthened, as the two stared each other down.

After an eon, Sela, tired of Hel's intrusion into her sleep, spat waspishly, "What in the name of that lunatic to whom you grovel do you want? Really, Hel, it eludes me as to why you kiss the ass of the very deity who banished you to the bowels of Helheim."

"I have no time to waste bickering with you, whore. I am here to convey a simple message. If you stay with my father, you will be the cause of his death. If that happens, I shall hold you personally responsible. I do not care that you rid Helheim of Peer. Anything he made you suffer in the pit will seem like an afternoon's picnic compared with what I shall inflict on you."

"Yeah, yeah, yeah. How many times have you threatened me?" Sela retaliated.

Given how often Hel tried to intimidate Sela with dire warnings, she doubted Hel was capable of making good on any of them or that she was even woman enough to try.

"Next time, you hag-born moldwarp, send me an email and stay out of my dreams."

Sela banished Hel by opening her eyes, relieved to hear the steady rhythm of Loki's sleep apnea reverberating around the room.

"One day, old man, I'm gonna get you one of those CPAP machines to cure your mating calls, but until then snore away, husband."

She shuffled onto her back and stared at the ceiling, blankly. Questions flooded her brain, banishing any hope of sleep.

Why did the realms despise her unborn child to the point of death?

What was happening to Loki, and why was Hel so sure he was going to die?

The biggest question being, *how could she prevent it?*

As forecast, by sunrise the storm had blown over and the Canadian road crews had earned their pay. The main roads cleared enough to be described as passable.

Surprisingly, given the unwanted visitor in her dreams,

Sela had fallen asleep shortly before dawn. As the morning sunlight peeked through the threadbare curtains, the beam hit Sela's eyes to guarantee she did not stay that way for long.

Grudgingly, her eyes flitted open, the first thought in her groggy brain was Loki. Concerned for his health, Sela wriggled under the covers to check her husband.

Despite a full night's sleep, he looked pale and haggard.

As for the baby, its rhythmic kicks demanded Sela eat before they set out on their thirty-hour journey.

Braving the lukewarm shower, she dressed quickly hoping *not* to contract pneumonia from the chill in the room, grimacing when she saw her movements had not disturbed Loki. She frowned at the thought of waking him, but they had to hit the road without delay.

"I'm sorry, my love. Needs must," she murmured, sounding anything but apologetic. Climbing onto the bed, she marshalled her strength and shoved Loki off the mattress, smirking when he hit the floor with an ungainly thump.

"Was that really necessary?" A deep voice, reverting to Norse, grunted the question into the carpeting.

"Hmm, maybe not, but it was funny. Even you can't deny that."

"I would love to know which demon in Helheim taught you about humor."

"I'd have to say everything I learned, I learned from you."

"Remind me to have a serious talk to myself about my skewed sense of logic."

"How about you get your butt off the floor to feed your wife and child."

"Yeah, yeah, right away," Loki muttered drowsily, fingers digging into the comforter, ostensibly to pull himself up."

Wise to this ruse, Sela tugged on the other side of the comforter. "No, you don't. You are not going to curl yourself up in it and go back to sleep."

"Vixen," Loki chastised his wife for outwitting him.

"And you love me for it."

On his feet and dressed, Loki offered his arm to Sela. "Shall we?"

At a nod from his wife, the pair tempted fate by risking breakfast at the attached diner.

Sitting in the booth across from her husband who, more or less, ignored her rants about the hospitality industry, Sela posted a scathing review about the motel where they had just spent the night.

Loki looked over his menu. "I wish that idiot child had not taught you about apps."

"Hey, you wanted me to have this damnable nuisance."

"Only to keep track of you. That you would figure out how to use the actual phone never mind the added extras was not part of the bargain. Do you know how much unlimit—"

Loki curbed his lecture when Sela put her phone down to study her menu.

"Tough cookies." She blew him a kiss, watching him peruse the 'delights' on offer. She hoped he wanted one of everything listed, as was his habit, but all he ordered was coffee and toast.

Sela, on the other hand, slightly embarrassed, ordered three eggs and a small steak, in addition to bacon and hash browns.

When the food was delivered, Loki smiled, although it lacked his familiar twinkle and, to Sela's well-concealed consternation, only picked at his toast.

Before he could rib her, Sela said, "Don't say a word. It's not my fault your child has your appetite."

He chuckled softly. "Good thing I can still afford to feed you, otherwise, you'd be scrubbing pots and pans for the next week to pay for that meal."

Grinning impishly, Sela stuck out her tongue before devouring everything on her plate. By the end of the meal, the baby was satisfied and settled down — to Sela's relief.

Their long journey north began.

The sun glistened off the fresh, powdery snow, the scene reminiscent of glitter-covered Christmas cards — another source of fascination to Sela, who dug out a pair of sunglasses from the glove box to counter the glare.

The blizzard meant they had no choice but to stay on the Trans-Canada Highway. Sela remained alert not only to what lay ahead, but also what might be sneaking up behind as the coupe burned through the seemingly endless expanse of Canada.

They stopped outside Quebec City long enough for gas and snacks. Sela was determined to force something into Loki, uncaring whether that was junk food.

His waistline is the least of my worries.

She knew it was impossible for him to get fat, envying him, his metabolism.

Returning to the Highway, Sela pushed the coupe as hard and fast as she could without drawing the interest of the law... or the valkyries.

SEVEN

The valkyries were too busy dealing with their own problems to worry about what was unfolding in the northern climes of Midgard.

Svipul paced her room angrily, visualizing every torturous form of death she could inflict on Odin for what he had done to Hodor.

Thoughts of snakes poisoning his wretched body then feasting on his rotting corpse, *or* the old deity being stampeded by a herd of wild moose, their hooves decimating his bones.

While tempting, her deliberations generated only the briefest of pleasure.

No, none of those methods would suffice. She had to be certain Odin's death was successful and at *her* hands.

Lost in her plans, she failed to hear either the knock on her door or the entrance of Herja and Brynhildr.

Bryn paused just inside the door, letting Herja tiptoe closer.

"Svi?" Herja's measured tones interrupted her twin's rumination, bringing her back to reality.

Being born minutes apart does not, necessarily, equate to a lifetime of affinity, but Svi and Herja had been inseparable since their unceremonious arrival into the world, and remained the closest of the sisters who made up the valkyries.

It amused and saddened Svipul that, although Herja was blessed with a soothing voice and profound beauty, she was also cursed with the responsibility of delivering unmitigated devastation.

Svipul turned to find her twin within inches of her. Out of habit and love for Herja, she paused long enough to give her a hug.

Glancing over Herja's shoulder, Svipul smiled at Bryn, inclining her head in tacit acknowledgement of her support.

Breaking the embrace, gently, Herja repeated her pleas for Svipul to abandon her wrath. She feared her sister's anger was no match for Odin's insanity.

"Please, little one, I know how much you loved Hodor, but this is madness."

"Madness, Herja? You, of all the sisters, should know how dangerous uncontrolled destruction can be. That imbecile's reign needs to be terminated before his lunacy destroys us all."

"But Svi, his time is coming—" Herja started.

"To an end, my beloved twin?" dryly, Svi stopped her. "Do you believe that? Even with my gift of foresight, I cannot see the fate awaiting the old fool. He has done well having Myst shroud it. No, my dear heart, I must eradicate him myself. That none are permitted to wield their powers in the Hall works in our favour."

A second, softer voice chimed in.

Suppressed sobs laced Bryn's words. "Svi, please listen

to Herja. You know what Odin did to me for offending him.

"You have no idea the extent of loneliness and torment I suffered in that castle before Sigurðr saved me, and still I was stripped of my powers with no hope of regaining them.

"*My* heinous crime? Allowing the wrong king to die in battle. I could not possibly imagine what he would do to you if you failed to kill him."

"So, he chops me into little pieces and dispatches me to Helheim," Svi snarled. "At least I will be reunited with the true owner of my heart."

Svipul's eyes brimmed with tears. "I refuse to endanger either of you in the actual attack, but I beg you to help me in this. My head is boiling with contempt and enmity, preventing me from thinking straight."

The other two gathered their sister into a warm embrace. They could no more deny Svi her vengeance than they could stop her from acting alone.

While Herja might prefer to stay this way for eternity, plans had to be made to rid the realms of Odin.

Dawn approached, the final elements were in the hands of Svi and Herja.

Bryn had vanished from Valhalla before Odin registered her presence. Her banishment was supposed to be permanent; to be caught flouting the decree meant immediate execution.

"Are we set, Herja?" Svipul tried to sound confident, but the pair knew failure would result in consequences neither could imagine.

Herja blew a sigh, "Yes, my little one, we are. I will ensure Odin is waiting in the Great Hall. I beg you to reconsider. You stand a better chance with the protection of all the sisters. To challenge alone is pure—"

Svipul raised her palm.

"No more, Herja. You know we cannot trust all the sisters. Odin has too many who serve him heedlessly," she took Herja's hands in hers, "and besides this is *my* fate. It is the only way."

She mustered up a reassuring smile.

"At least let me be present to see he is destroyed beyond his magic," Herja pleaded, blinking hard so as not to weep.

"Once my dagger has done its job, Herja, you may dispose of his body as you see fit," Svipul prevaricated, keenly aware, if she was successful, she would not stop hacking at Odin until nothing remained of his evil infested corpse.

Needing time alone, Svipul kissed Herja on the cheek and sent her to her own room.

The usual party in the Hall dragged on through the day and into the night.

Svipul did not leave her room for any of the festivities, preferring to listen, while sharpening her dagger.

She could hear the old man's peals of increasingly drunken laughter as the hours wore on.

Svi watched as the shadows of time crept across her wall.

She let the dying light of day catch the edge of her

blade. The beam danced over the finely honed weapon, bringing a satisfied smile to her lips.

The din from the Hall softened little by little as the crowd began to disperse.

Since Freya was nowhere to be found, Svipul suspected Herja had assumed the duties of hostess to make sure the party was a *success*.

She also knew her twin would be herding the others out as quickly as possible.

Even with Herja's skilled insistence, it was well past moonrise when the last few sycophants departed, still carousing raucously.

Svipul heard the sisters clearing the remains of the party from the Hall.

How that menial task became the valkyries' responsibility, I shall never be able to fathom.

"One more reason for him to die," she hissed.

The dwindling rattle of plates and goblets signaled it was time for Svipul to leave her room.

Her ear pressed to the door, Svipul heard the insignificant discussion between Odin and Herja regarding the evening's revelry.

She paid scant heed to its content, but used it to mark the position of the pair within the room, concluding Herja was on the other side of the door waiting to exit, while the old fool was talking into the fireplace as was his habit.

Unfortunately for Svipul, this meant she had to cross the Hall to reach him.

As planned, the door swung open, Herja calling a farewell to Odin loudly enough to mask Svipul's entrance. Herja slipped past her sister, leaving the two alone in the room.

Her senses on high alert, Herja had intended to leave the heavy oak door slightly ajar, prepared to spring into action to assist her twin should it prove necessary.

Her underlying unease about this whole plan, blossomed into alarm when she heard the faint creak of the hinge as the door settled into the jamb, followed by the muted thunk of the bolt sliding into place.

Herja's heart sank. Her mind whirling, she turned and leaned against the door. Bad enough Odin had decreed the Hall to be magic free — now this damned door had become an almost impenetrable barrier.

Conscious of how well Odin could hold his mead, Herja prayed the herbs with which she had laced his drinks might be enough to dull his reactions. Svipul needed only seconds to exact her revenge.

Svipul studied the old man, her eyes darkening with an implacable revulsion. She drew her blade, knuckles white as she clutched the handle.

Attacking Odin at a run was out of the question, leaving her one alternative.

In a single, powerful bound, her massive silver-tinged wings unfurled to propel her across the floor.

Her dagger in both hands, Svipul was intent on plunging it as deep into the bastard's back as possible, only to have the downwards arc of the knife halt abruptly as stars filled her eyes.

Svipul found herself struggling helplessly in a grip that

tightened around her throat. She lashed out blindly with her blade, but it was knocked from her hands, clattering to the floor.

Trapped like a bird in a net, Svipul refused to give up the fight, hearing a scathing cackle at her desperate attempt to break free.

The bitter stench of alcohol on the All Father's breath made her retch as he berated, "You stupid bitch. Do you think you are the only one in this Hall who can foresee the future? I knew what was in your mind since the day I destroyed that weakling Hodor."

Svipul gasped for air as, in his wrath, Odin shook her by her throat until her teeth rattled.

"I was beginning to think you had come to your senses. Regrettably, you are as great an imbecile as your lover."

Odin yanked her closer to his lips. He wanted to make sure she didn't miss a word.

"I guarantee you, valkyrie, no winged whore with a toy knife will have the satisfaction of killing me."

Nimbly, the Asgardian spun the slender valkyrie in his immense hand.

Svipul trembled when she felt her feathers being crushed together as they were caught between her body and Odin's. The fire in his breath burned her ear as his voice lowered to a malevolent growl.

"I will make sure you do not disappoint your lover in the afterlife with your failures, as well."

With a swift flick of his wrist, Odin ripped Svipul's left wing from her back.

The scream erupting from her throat echoed throughout Valhalla as her body convulsed violently in his hold. Blood flowed down her spine from the gaping hole he left behind.

Odin discarded her bloody appendage in the fire and, before she could recover, he repeated the gesture with her remaining wing.

Svipul went limp in Odin's hand.

"Oh the irony. You are able to predict the demise of entire realms... but, by letting your heart rule your head, miss your own. Witless fool." He barked a spiteful laugh.

From the moment the bolt barred entry to the Hall, Herja knew their plot was destined to fail.

Stranded on the other side of the door, she threw herself bodily against the unforgiving wood - a futile endeavor which only served to bruise her shoulders.

She persevered until, inexplicably and without warning, the door gave way.

The sheer force of her momentum sent her tumbling across the floor, into the middle of the macabre scene.

Scrambling to her feet, Herja readied herself to cast a spell powerful enough to destroy the entire realm.

"Do you really want your sister's death to be on your conscience, Herja?" Odin mocked as he dangled Svipul's body from his mighty grip.

Slowly, Herja lowered her hands, dispelling the magic she had summoned.

Aghast, she averted her gaze, her stomach rebelling.

The once beautiful, silver sheen of Svipul's wing — the balance to Herja's own gilt hued feathers; gifted at their birth by the *Norns... the Fates* — was sullied by congealing, ugly red streaks.

To Herja's horror, the dying wing flapped frantically as though searching for its owner; its misery extinguished when Odin cast it in the fire as carelessly as he had discarded the remnants of his meal.

Bile roast in Herja's throat at the sickening crackle of the feathers igniting.

"Look at her, witch," Odin demanded of Herja.

Unconsciously, her eyes responded to Odin's exhortation, transfixed by the sight of her twin's tear-stained face and the rivers of blood pouring down her body.

Herja's heart shattered at Svipul's whimpered plea for her sister to save herself, the words disjointed by moans of excruciating pain.

Terror coiled through her when she saw Odin pull his mighty sword from its sheath.

"Please, Odin. Please have mercy on her," Herja beseeched. "She was distraught by the death of her love and, deranged by grief, lost her senses. She would not dare attack otherwise."

"*Silence*," Odin commanded, "Now I have your full attention, you'll be happy to know I do not intend to kill our misguided Svipul here. Unfortunately, she is of no use to me anymore... and neither are you."

Odin dipped his blade into the fire. A brilliant flame, the likes of which Herja had never witnessed, erupted.

Before she could blink, he tossed Svipul into the massive grate. Her body vanished instantly.

The blatant injustice of Odin flouting his own rules, fanned Herja's torment, acutely aware she had no defence against his insanity.

"You promised not to kill her," Herja screamed in anguish, sure the blaze had consumed her sister's body.

Smiling, although there was no humor in it, Odin stepped away from the fireplace. "I assure you she still lives, but I neither know, nor care to where or when the flames delivered her. If you wish to save her, the onus is on you to find her."

Odin gestured to the dying flame. "I suggest you make your decision quickly."

Herja rushed towards the smoldering embers.

No sooner had her foot struck the hearth than she felt a tug on her gilded wings, nearly knocking her off her feet.

Hauled backwards, she was swivelled around with a speed that made her giddy, until she faced the god to whom she had once sworn absolute fealty, but whose reason had been ravaged by madness.

The fury-filled gaze with which Herja pinned Odin, would have quailed a lesser deity.

Her acrimony elicited nothing more than a derisive curl of his lips. He leveled the blade at her eyes, and almost purred when he passed his judgment, "Riddle me this... how does a sightless valkyrie control the destruction she wreaks?"

Panic-stricken, Herja squirmed, cold dread chilling her to the bone.

Odin taunted, "Was she worth the price?"

EIGHT

As the miles sped by in a continuous blur of trees and cities, the pair turned east, stopping only when necessary. Sela was determined to push both her car and her body to their limits.

The previous day had cruised into a long and, thankfully, uneventful night alleviated only by broken white lines zipping past the Ford's running board.

The monotonous pattern became soporific, and Sela zoned out occasionally, quickly catching herself. She resorted to winding down the window, the frigid air keeping her awake.

The tedious darkness was hewn, by the touch of a brilliant sunrise, into a new day.

Oblivious to nature's glory, Sela's eyes were fixed on the road, acutely aware, if she stayed in one place too long, they would be discovered by the realms.

The uncertainty of what lay at their journey's end tormented her, an issue compounded by how, and to what extent, Hel and Freya were involved in this madness.

Convinced her visions related to Freya, Sela believed the

goddess would stop at nothing to kill, or worse — steal the babe. If Freya couldn't bear Loki's child, she would settle for appropriating one by fair means or foul.

While that suspicion tended to elicit a twinge of fear, *this* twinge was something more, and Sela was unable to suppress a scream at the sudden, wrenching pain in her stomach.

Laboring to keep her car from straying into the ditch, she braked hard and pulled to the side of the road. Even as she trembled in agony, Loki's defensive driving courses allowed her to bring the car to a halt safely.

Suffering from Braxton Hicks contractions during her pregnancy, Sela had grown used to the regular assaults on her body, something which prompted her doctor to recommend bed rest until the child was born.

Loki had convinced the pediatrician that, unless he was suggesting chaining Sela to the bed, she would never stay there and perhaps the proposed exercise routine might suit her better.

Against his better judgment, the doctor was persuaded.

Loki had a way with people — aided and abetted by his ability to control their thoughts.

This pain was unlike anything she had experienced thus far.

A second, more powerful cramp bit into her lower abdomen before the first subsided, and she grabbed Loki's arm, her nails gouged his skin, drawing blood.

"Damn you, Loki, wake up," Sela shrieked.

The command was unnecessary. Loki had been woken by the gratuitous removal of flesh from his bicep.

"What is it? Are we being attacked by the valkyrie or Odin's Chariot, maybe?" Scanning their surroundings, Loki added snidely, "Scared of a stray moose?"

"Loki, could you be serious, for once in your life? I'm going into labor, you numbskull. For your information, wise guy, the only animal more dangerous than a hippo is a Canadian moose."

Loki arched a brow at his wife and raked his eyes over her.

Sela swore the bastard was trying to stifle a grin. She contemplated reaching for her blade to remove his head when another contraction hit her.

"Do something constructive you shag-haired, toad spotted, horse drench, or our baby will be born in the front seat of this caaaaaaarrrrrr..." Sela's words swallowed in a howl.

Loki placed his hand on Sela's bulge, feeling the movement and counted silently.

Satisfied, he nodded and informed her in his most soothing voice, "No, my love, it's not quite time yet, but you might want to drive faster, because our child does not intend to wait much longer."

"*Drive faster*? How am I supposed to drive at all with the creature from Helheim trying to tear me apart? We need a hospital *now*," Sela panted.

Loki curved his hand across her stomach again. Instantly, the pain decreased.

"A Midgard hospital cannot help us, Sel. We must get to Newfoundland. The child agreed to a brief... err... postponement, brief being the operative word."

Sela inhaled a deep breath as the last of the contractions dissipated.

Confused, her eyes locked with those of her husband, but her question died on her lips when flashing lights reflected in the rearview mirror broke the moment.

The lanky figure of a highway patrolman appeared at Sela's door before she could wind the window down.

"Nice car, ma'am," the patrolman complemented as he performed a cursory inspection of the occupants.

"License and registration, please."

Sela produced the requested documents from her purse.

"Is there a problem, officer?" she asked in dulcet tones.

"It's unusual to find a car stopped on the side of the road...with New York plates, no less. I am not doing my job properly if I don't stop to investigate, and I'm pretty sure my partner would be very upset if he found out I left a woman here in the middle of nowhere. Especially one who is pregnant and alone."

Sela glanced in the mirror to see his partner sitting in their car, talking to someone on the radio. She assumed he was running her plates.

The curious way the patrolman emphasized the word *alone,* snapped Sela's eyes back to him.

"Alone? I assure you, officer, my husband is..." she twisted in her seat to see a large wolf where Loki had been sitting. The hair on Sela's arms prickled, the creature's deep blue eyes warning her trouble was afoot.

"Are you okay, ma'am? Have you been drinking?" the patrolman pressed.

"No, officer. I have not been drinking. I guess I'm a little tired after driving all night. If there is nothing else, I can do for you, I will be on my..."

"Please secure your dog, ma'am, and step out of the car." The cop did not appear to be listening to Sela.

Sela checked her mirror to see his colleague alight from the passenger side of the patrol car.

He was a shorter, stockier cop and, oddly, his uniform didn't fit properly. He took up position at the rear of her car, his hand on his pistol.

Plastering a smile on her face, she looked at the cop hovering by her window. "You know, sir, I'm not feeling very well and an escort to the next city might—"

"Ma'am, I've already asked you once to exit the vehicle," he reiterated in a no-nonsense tone *"Do not* make me tell you again."

Sela noticed he had flipped the clasp on his holster and was poised to draw his gun.

Unwilling to give him that chance, Sela reached for the door handle. "There's no need for trouble, officer. I'm more than happy to oblige."

Her hand froze at a deep growl from the wolf next to her, and she realized he had been watching the second patrolman in the passenger mirror.

The cop who had crept along the vehicle, was now at the passenger-side door.

Loki bared his teeth; his snarl, a clear message **not** to open her door.

"Ma'am, muzzle your dog before I have to shoot it," the first officer ordered.

"Like Hell you're going to shoot my dog," Sela yelled.

The cop's fingers curled around his weapon.

Sela kicked open her door, sending him sprawling onto the pavement. She turned in time to see Loki press himself through solid metal to materialize on the road in front of the second cop.

The giant wolf lunged, his fangs sinking deep into a flabby throat.

In a single bite, Loki removed the patrolman's head.

Sela heard the *whump* of it hitting the rear windscreen, smearing a trail of blood down the glass. In awed fascination she was transfixed by her husband's skill as he rounded the back of the car, towards the first patrolman.

The distinct click of a Smith and Wesson 9mm pistol chambering a round jerked her gaze to the spread-eagled officer.

Trying to draw a bead on the wolf, the cop shuffled onto his side, gaping goggle-eyed at his partner's blood. Globules trailed from the powerful jaws of the beast now seeking to tear him apart.

Sela saw his hand trembling as he tried to aim, his finger white with the pressure on the trigger.

Bang!

The first shot exploded from the 9mm's barrel.

Fortunately for Loki, it went wild when Sela delivered a swift kick, her Doc Martins pitching the patrolman onto his back.

He tried to swing the gun at her, only to catch sight of Sela's glittering dagger, the tip of the blade plunging deep into his jugular before he could fire the second round.

Dropping his gun, the cop clutched at his throat in an attempt to staunch the blood. A pointless exercise.

Loki launched his own attack.

Pinning the man to the asphalt, Loki ripped him to pieces.

The carnage the wolf rained down on the lifeless body was too much even for Sela.

Blessed silence descended.

A hand came to rest on Sela's shoulder.

At first, she was afraid to look, certain it was the remains of the cop returning to haunt her.

The warm voice in her ear put that fear to rest, "*Hér, ástin mín*, you do not want to lose your dagger."

Loki slipped the blade into her boot holster.

Sela faced her blood-drenched mate. "Was that really necessary, Loki? Did you have to make a meal out of him?"

Loki cast an eye at the mutilated carcass. "Let's just say I wanted to leave a message."

Angered by his recklessness, Sela punched him in the chest. "You do realize, you *hálfviti*, the entire Canadian Law Enforcement System will be on the look-out for us. Did you happen to think of that?"

Loki snagged the one tattered piece of the officer's uniform which had escaped his canines.

Wiping his face with it, he shrugged. "I doubt it. I'm sure no one will miss these two. 'Sides, they aren't human. They're elves, or at least they were."

"***Elves***?" Sela stared at the corpse. "Aren't they supposed to be small with pointy ears? How can you tell?"

"They stink." Loki chuckled. "I guess it's from frolicking around so much in their damn magical forest... who knows."

"Why didn't they just kill us when they had the chance? I mean they had several opportunities," Sela asked, totally baffled by the turn of events.

She looked up to see Loki walking back to where the patrol car was parked. Following, she watched him scour the vehicle.

"Are you going to answer me? Why didn't they just kill us and be done with it? And what the hell are you looking for?" She all but stamped her frustration that Loki was ignoring her.

Finally, he gave her an answer.

"Because, my love... ahhh." Pausing long enough to

retrieve what he was searching for. "Just as I suspected." Loki turned and faced his wife, dangling two sets of ancient-looking handcuffs in front of her nose.

"I think their plan was to take us alive to use as leverage with Odin. Seems the old Asgardian may not have as much control of the realms as he thinks."

"How could a simple set of cuffs be any good to them? You're Loki, God of Mischief and who really knows what else?" Sela asked somewhat mockingly, hoping it might trigger a further conversation.

Loki sidestepped her question. "They are steeped in a powerful, almost primeval, magic. How these two came across them, I can only guess. In any case, they have the ability to absorb even my magic, or at least weaken it severely," Loki explained.

He winked at Sela as he tossed her the cuffs. "Who knows, we might have some fun with these. Is it wrong to say these kinda make me horny?"

He waggled his brows, and sent her a lascivious smile.

She threw the cuffs back. "Really, Loki? I'm about ready to drop, we've just been attacked by yet another realm, and all you can think about is sex?"

Exasperated, Sela heaved a long-suffering sigh and stalked back to her car. "Join me when you grow up so we can get out of here."

Sela climbed into the car and watched for her husband in the mirror.

With a wave of his hand, he cleared the site of the car and bodies, the cuffs now hooked to his belt.

Loki slid into the car next to Sela, a silly grin on his face.

Sela rolled her eyes. "I don't know what's worse, raising one child... or *two*."

Putting the car into gear, they sped off into the sunrise.

NINE

They arrived at the North Sydney terminal in time to catch the midnight ferry to Newfoundland.

Relieved they had made it — notwithstanding her fatigue, which resulted in her veering off the road an uncomfortable number of times, scarcely avoiding at least five ditches — Sela was especially thankful she no longer had to listen to Loki's execrable attempts to sing along with the French version of *Highway to Hell* playing, inexplicably, on every radio station.

Glad to get out of the car, Sela stretched her tired legs. She had shied away from checking the rear-view mirror for the last few hours because she didn't want to see the dark circles under her eyes.

Conscious it was an impossibility, did not stop her trying to rub them away.

She filled her lungs with the salty air of the ocean, a scent she found intoxicating. The lights from the boats bobbing in the harbor banished grim memories of recent days.

Unexpectedly, she had a warm sense of being close to

home, despite knowing her real home was thousands of miles away... not to mention over a thousand years in the past.

Loki smiled as he watched his wife, pleased to see her relax, albeit temporarily.

He went into the office to book their passage along with her damn car, cursing inwardly for buying her the rolling garbage can; simultaneously, conceding it made her happy.

For all the times during his existence when he had failed to consider anyone but himself, that single gift had been a crowning moment of glory.

Normally, the ferry would be full of tourists traveling to the rugged beauty of Newfoundland, but so early in the season the load was light and Loki secured a small berth for the two of them.

He hoped Sela would sleep for the entire seven hours it would take to reach the island, while he spent the trip ensuring they didn't have any unannounced company.

Spotting Sela leaning on the railing staring out to sea, he walked over and looped his arm around her waist.

Resting her head against his side, she murmured, "It's beautiful, isn't it?"

Bending to brush a kiss on her soft, thick curls, Loki replied just as quietly, "Almost as beautiful as the Norse Lands."

Sela smiled up at him, aware that although he could read her mind, he rarely had to; he knew her too well.

Loki held her a little tighter adding, almost inaudibly, "Though this place is nothing like it used to be."

The horn, announcing it was time to embark, interrupted the moment and prevented Sela from quizzing Loki about his cryptic comment.

The pair climbed back into the coupe and drove to the ferry.

On board, Sela harried the deckhand in charge of loading the vehicles until he thought he was about to have a heart attack.

Even with the near empty cargo hold, she was sure some idiot would bang a door into her paint job and leave an irreparable scratch. She coerced the poor man into rearranging all the vehicles so her precious car sat by itself, straddling two spots.

For all his craft and guile, Loki could not fathom how she got away with that.

Listening intently, he was amused by her methods of persuasion.

Her negotiating talents were more threats of bodily injury than tact and diplomacy.

Once Sela had choreographed things to her satisfaction, she scanned the clutter of parked cars. None of which held a candle to her beautiful coupe, sitting in splendid isolation.

A dark vehicle in the far corner piqued her interest, but she could not be bothered to walk across to have a nosy.

"There, now was that so hard?" she mused when she rejoined her husband.

"Not once you stop promising to remove his balls and feed them to him, love. I'm sure clarity lit the way at that point.

"Come on, I spent our last coin on a bed, and you look like you could definitely use it."

"Always the charmer." Sela elbowed Loki in his gut, making him chuckle.

Lifting his wife into his arms, he carried her as though she was the finest crystal, wending his way to the berths, oblivious of their fellow passengers' curious glances.

By the time Sela and Loki reached their cabin, the final horn announced the ferry's imminent departure.

Sela watched through the porthole in childlike wonder as they slid away from the jetty and out through the harbor.

Passing the collection of fishing trawlers, pleasure craft, and cabin cruisers, she marveled at the stories each one must hold, imagining the voyages and ports of call they had seen.

Straining to see the boats as the last of the harbor lights dimmed from view, Sela gave up and joined her husband in bed.

Curling into the crook for his arm, she mumbled on a yawn, "You really do know how to show a woman a good time at sea, dontcha, sailor."

Before Loki could think of a witty comeback, he heard her breathing slow as she dozed off.

He didn't move until he was sure she was fast asleep. Hearing the soft wheeze of the snores Sela denied she made, Loki slid from the bed and out of the cabin.

As Sela sank into a deeper slumber, her mind was inundated by a flurry of dreams.

Each bore its own message, but none were menacing enough to jolt her awake.

One was more detailed, bore more weight, and was not so much a dream as a memory from long ago.

In the dream, Sela glimpsed her reflection in a pond. She looked about seven or eight.

Scanning the landscape, she recognized her village; a bundle of longhouses nestled together in a clearing not far from where she stood. Unable to suppress a smile, she skipped to where she knew her mother and father would be busy tending the herds.

During her millennia in Hell and her time on Earth, Sela had discerned naught but a hint of her family in her dreams. Now, she was home and couldn't wait to see them... to hug them.

The sun was warm, the breeze light, and the herds were grazing in the clearing. On the face of it, everything appeared normal, typically tranquil... but something was not quite right.

Her parents were nowhere around. Odd, her father would not leave the animals unattended... unless...

Her mother's screams rent the air.

Sela could not pinpoint where they were coming from, but she raced to the longhouse.

Bursting through the doorway, she saw her father kneeling on the floor.

His broad back was towards Sela, making it impossible to see his face. In front of him, her mother was splayed on the ground; but Sela could not see her face either.

"*Sela*."

She jumped at her father's stentorian tone.

"Run and fetch the *völva*. Tell her your mother is about to give birth, but there is something wrong with the baby."

Her mother's screams chased the little girl from the house, and she ran in search of the witch, yelling her name.

While the entire community held the old woman in high regard for her healing powers, the grizzled hag scared Sela. She believed, while the woman *did* practice good magic, she also wielded a magic far more dangerous and deadly than any in the village dared mention.

Sela found the old healer wandering through the woods, collecting berries and herbs for her potions. Swallowing her fear for the sake of her mother's life, she raced to the woman and snagged her sleeve, pulling on it as hard as she could.

"Please, you must come now," Sela begged. "The baby... my papa sent... my mama... hurry, pleeeeease."

Sela babbled incoherently, words tumbling from her lips like a spring waterfall.

The older woman paused in her task to study the little girl. Her gentle smile appeared to be matched by an understanding sparkle in her eyes.

The warmth in the woman's voice enveloped Sela, alleviating her alarm.

"Calm yourself, my child, and tell me what has you in such a panic?"

Sela gulped in a breath.

"It is my mama, *völva*. Papa sent me because something's wrong with the baby. Mama is in pain and needs your help."

The old woman listened to the girl for a moment, then shrugged and returned to her chores.

Crouching to pick some ground ivy for her arthritis potion, she explained, "It is an omen, little one, nature's way. The baby is not right and must die... it is unfortunate that your mother must die as well, but there is nothing I can do to prevent that."

Sela stared at the woman in disbelief.

Horrified, she beat her small fists against the uncaring witch's back. Tears streamed down her cheeks, she protested, "This is what you do. You heal people, you save their lives. How can you ignore them and let my mother and sister die?"

"Sister?" the woman asked without turning. "Are you sure it was your mother and your sister?"

Sela stopped hitting the old woman, registering her question.

Yes, it had to be her sister.

She remembered the day her sister was born, recalled wandering into the house, even though her father had ordered her to stay out. Watching her mother give birth to the baby girl — but her sister was delivered without any complications. In fact, the family had always joked she simply walked out.

"Tell me, child, is it your mother who is in danger or you? Are not your mother and father long dead, as well as your brothers and sisters?"

"Stop," Sela wailed. "I just saw them. They are in the house, they need you. Oh, please."

The *völva* wiped her hands on her skirt, and faced the hysterical girl. Gathering Sela in her arms, she hugged her close.

The all too familiar voice sent chills through the dream-forged eight-year-old.

"It is too late for you to prevent what's about to happen, but you must finish your journey.

"Now, wake up..."

The voice insisted she wake up, only the tone and timbre had changed.

"Wake up, Sela. ***Sela, wake up***."

She felt hands shaking her by her shoulders, dragging her from her dream.

Gasping, tears spilling down her cheeks, Sela blinked awake to see Loki sitting on the edge of the bunk next to her.

Needing comfort and protection, she bolted upright and clung to him, burying her face in his chest, trying to steady herself.

"My baby is going to die and so am I. Freya told me." To Sela, the message was unequivocal.

"*Freya?*" Loki questioned. "Sweetheart, it was just a dream. It's natural for expectant mothers to plan for the worst. I guarantee, where we are going, not even Freya can reach us."

Loki rocked her in his arms.

One day, Sela was going to ask Loki how he knew so much about expectant mothers. Moreover, she wanted to know just how many of his offspring there were, but now wasn't the time.

"She said..." Sela needed to make Loki understand that Freya could find them anywhere.

"Your imagination told you, Sela. It was a dream and nothing more."

Loki kissed the top of her head as though with so simple a gesture he could he banish her nightmares. He chuckled softly. "Besides, the worst fear you should be having is whether you're going to be a terrible parent?"

Sela thumped him for that crack.

"A parenting joke from the guy whose daughter was

raised to run Helheim. That's the definition of good child rearing."

He ignored her dig. "The sun is beginning to rise. Why don't you come on to the upper deck with me and watch it? If you look towards the horizon, you might be able to make out the harbor lights of the port where we're about to dock."

Loki relaxed his bear hug and got to his feet, offering his hand to Sela. "I promise you, Freya is nowhere to be seen."

TEN

Skillfully, the captain maneuvered the ferry through the throng of craft cluttering Port aux Basques harbor as the port woke to face the hustle and bustle of the new day.

The fishing fleets were preparing to sail out to the open seas in search of the day's catch. Captains of the armada of tourist boats hoped there were enough rich suckers on the incoming ferry to make the day worthwhile.

Gripping the wooden railing, Sela's knuckles grew whiter at the sight of the ferry's approaching berth.

Nausea lurked, increasing with every passing second. She chalked it up to being a pregnant woman on a boat, suffering from the worst case of seasickness in recorded history.

That the end of this mysterious road trip loomed like the void she had escaped, added an unadulterated dread to the mix, exacerbating her late-term morning sickness.

The ferry's horn announced their arrival into port, quickly followed by the annoyed voice of the deckhand from the hold.

"Would the owner of the *classic* Ford please report to the vehicle deck. You are blocking traffic."

Loki grinned at Sela. "I think you're being paged."

There was no humor in Sela's eyes when they met his.

"He can damn well wait, Loki. I'm not taking one more step, let alone getting back into that car, until you tell me why you dragged me halfway across Canada to this particular island? How could this possibly be any more protected than New York?" Her voice had lost all its color.

The frustrated breath which filled Loki's lungs seemed to reverberate throughout the harbor, almost drowning out the constant droning of the deckhand still looking for, **"the owner of the piece of shit, to get her ass below before I push it overboard."**

Exhaling, Loki answered Sela with a question, "Do you know where you are?"

"According to the harbor sign, this is Port aux Basques, Newfoundland. Big deal, that doesn't clear up anything." Sela was tired of Loki's games. "Please, just tell me why we are here, or I'm going back to the City."

"Are you aware of the history of this island?" Loki pressed.

"Yes, I've watched enough documentaries to know that Leif Eriksson beat Columbus to the New World by landing at L'Anse aux Meadows."

She flung out of Loki's arms, turning her back to him.

"Vinland," Loki corrected, "and it was not by accident, Sela. He was directed there for a specific mission. Please, just trust me long enough to get us there. You'll understand more by seeing rather than me trying to explain."

Without moving, Sela replied, "I love you, Loki, but there are too many signs telling me I'll lose you if we do. I'd just as soon know you would stay alive if I left—"

"Don't you dare finish that thought." Now Loki's patience was being tested. "You do not get to make that decision."

Like a reprimanded child, Sela shoved past her husband and descended to the cargo bay.

Loki followed.

Neither spoke.

As the pair got into their vehicle, Sela treated the deck-hand to the universal one finger salute she had employed with gleeful frequency since her arrival in this accursed era.

Shoving the car into drive, she bolted down the ramp onto solid ground.

A horn blare from a blue and black car following her earned its driver the same gesture.

As for the faceless masses who might inadvertently step in front of the speeding coupe, they did so at their own risk.

Weaving her way through the plodding pedestrians, Sela shot up to Highway 1, and into the last few hours they might have together.

Not a word was shared for the first three hours of the drive.

Every time Loki opened his mouth, Sela's baleful glare curbed his tongue. He hated that look, but knew it was futile to say anything.

Reaching the off ramp to NL Route 430 just outside Deer Lake, Sela pulled off the road.

She was feeling weak and needed to get out of the car.

On unsteady feet, she leaned against the back fender, praying to any deity who did not want her dead at the moment, that she would not pass out.

Loki slid out of the car and joined her. "Are you ok?"

As the words left his mouth, he regretted asking the question.

"Really?" Sela fixed him with an *are you stupid* look. "Please, I need you to drive. I can't do it anymore."

Sela preferred to give birth in the driver's seat rather than trust her car to Loki, but she had no choice. She had been feeling gradually worse the longer they had been on the road.

This was more than being seasick or a case of anxiety. This was the onset of true labor and she needed her god-man to drive like the maniac he was so they might finish their quest.

Loki gawked at her as she trudged to the passenger side door.

He hesitated, unsure whether this was the best idea.

Sela had allowed him to drive her car once. It led to Loki losing his license as well as being forbidden from even sitting in the coupe.

To top it off, Sela had banned him from their bed.

It took all his charm and a week of sleeping on the couch before she forgave him.

If Sela wants me behind the wheel, it can only mean one thing...

There was no need to waste time standing there trying to answer the rhetorical question.

Awkwardly, Loki squeezed in without moving the seat.

The God of Chaos and Mischief swore at himself for being duped by the damn car yet again. Pushing back hard to adjust the position, he nearly jarred it from its track.

"Kindly do not break my car before you get the chance to run into something," Sela grumbled at him.

Loki ignored her long enough to get the seat right. Taking an extra second to blow a raspberry at his wife in childish petulance, he eased the Ford back onto the road cautiously.

Sela released a pain-wracked scream, and Loki pressed the accelerator to the floor.

Fortunately, for the entire province of Newfoundland, the traffic was light between Deer Lake and the Western Coast. Loki covered the forty-three miles to Rocky Harbour in a little over twenty minutes.

The coupe's engine light insisted he stop there.

Grudgingly, he let the car cool down, using the time to top up the radiator and make sure the baby wasn't crowning.

Satisfied with the condition of both, he continued the race north.

He knew Sela's precious car would be dead by the time they reached L'Anse aux Meadows, but he would deal with her wrath later.

The hundred-and-twenty-five-mile trip along the Western Coast was a mixture of wild beauty and quaint fishing villages, but neither Sela nor Loki noticed.

The scenery was nothing but a blur through the windshield and, somehow Loki did not draw the attention of the local constables and highway troopers.

Reaching Eddies Grove in a little over ninety minutes, he became aware of the faint but distinct odor of burning oil.

Neither despite the increasing discomfort of labor, had this gone unnoticed by Sela.

"What the hell are you doing to my car, you idiot?" she muttered in aggrieved Norse.

"I might be an idiot, and I'll buy you another car, wench, but right now you are more important than either," Loki retorted.

Sela groused at Loki about killing her car, for the next seventy-five miles, until they turned off onto Route 436 and the final stretch to Loki's mysterious destination.

At that moment, she fell eerily quiet.

The coupe bucked and fought with Loki every step of the way. The ravaged motor, Sela had so painstakingly restored to factory condition was on the verge of giving up the ghost.

It was only by the sheer force of will that he milked out the final few miles. The coupe refused to budge any further than the entrance to the Meadow.

Unfortunately for Loki, that wasn't where they needed to be.

Fighting his own exhaustion, Loki scooped Sela from the passenger side seat and began to run.

He was thankful the darkness concealed them from the ranger's station as they passed because, if it was manned, he did not have the strength or any magic left to do so himself.

He skirted the visitor's center and the ridiculous carvings of a Viking landing party, shaking his head, saddened that the once thriving community had been reduced to a tourist trap.

Unable to prevent progress, he ventured deeper into the park.

As Loki disappeared into the night, a second vehicle swung into the parking lot, cruised to a halt alongside the irreparable Ford, and doused its headlights immediately.

The sole occupant alighted and vented her fury on the coupe, finishing the annihilation Loki had started, for leading her on this madcap, not to mention storm ridden, cross-country pursuit.

Unbeknownst to any of the late night trespassers, her arrival and subsequent antics did *not* go unnoticed by the ranger monitoring the camera in the cabin, Loki had taken such pains to sneak past.

The alarm was raised.

Ahead, under the ethereal florescence of the full moon, Loki found the spot he was looking for.

The mound did not resemble those of the typical houses on the Meadows and, Loki surmised, the only reason it had been overlooked since the place had been *rediscovered*.

He rounded the far side of the mound and crumpled onto his knees. Sela was motionless in his arms and he feared the worst.

Reverting to Norse, Loki whispered a soft plea, "Bring us home."

Closing his eyes, he listened to the wind sough through the trees.

Suddenly, the sounds of voices using an ancient dialect not even Loki spoke any longer, filled the silence.

Opening his eyes, he saw life returning to the empty village.

Smoke, steeped in the scent of game and fish being prepared for the meal, billowed from the houses. Loki felt a hand gently but firmly grip his shoulder.

"Damn you, child, get the girl into my house now before we lose both of them."

The woman's voice brought hope to Loki but he wasn't sure even *she* could save his love.

She chided Loki as he shouldered his way through the door.

"You were supposed to be here days ago, but no. Just like your worthless father, you show up in your own sweet time.

"I swear, Loki—"

Tears flooded Loki's eyes as he faced her.

"Mother, not now," he begged. "You can curse my timing for the rest of eternity, but right now you need to save Sela.

"My magic is gone, and I can't help her."

ELEVEN

Under peril of death if he did not, Laufey persuaded her son to lay his unconscious, pregnant wife on the furs next to the fire.

Her next command was for him to vacate the premises.

That he did *both* without question was a good sign she was in control.

The last thing she needed, or desired, at this moment was to contend with his added chaos. She loved the boy, but at times, there were more reasons to murder him than there were stars in the sky.

"No time to ponder his idiosyncrasies... more pressing matters require my attention," Laufey explained to the unconscious woman on the furs.

Lying her hand on Sela's belly, Laufey waited to feel the babe move under her touch.

The child or rather her granddaughter, made a connection, and a wave of happiness swept through the old woman, though it was short lived.

Laufey realized her granddaughter was in the wrong position, and sensed she was finding it harder and harder to breathe. The umbilical cord had become entangled around the child's throat.

Laufey grabbed a small knife from her potions table and swirled the blade in a solution containing garlic to disinfect it.

She hoped the firebrand who had ensnared her son's heart would remain unconscious during the procedure she was about to perform, but imagined the likelihood was nil.

Scraping a dollop of dried clove-bud salve, Laufey slathered it over the Midgardian's flesh in an attempt to numb the incision as much as possible.

As Laufey prepared to make the first cut, Sela's eyes flew open.

Screaming for Loki, Sela threw a sucker punch, which caught the older woman by surprise. She tumbled backwards, the scalpel skidding across the floor.

Slightly dazed, Laufey scrambled to her knees scanning the floor for her missing blade. Her face ached, but she would deal with that later. Spying the blade under a chair, she scrabbled to retrieve it.

From the corner of her eye, she saw Sela struggling to get to her feet... presumably to beat her to it.

Determined to reach the scalpel before this wizened crone, Sela shrieked, "*Loki, help. Where are you?*"

"Loki," Laufey's irate summons spilled through the door, "get in here and restrain your woman before I slit her throat."

Loki burst into the house to see the two women grappling for control of the scalpel.

Sela was clutching Laufey's thick white hair and trying to slam the old woman's skull against the floor.

Defending herself, Laufey landed a couple of decent

blows to Sela's jaw in an attempt to render her unconscious.

The bright red mark blooming on Sela's chin... which would become a bruise soon enough... was matched by the blood tickling from the corner of her mouth.

Stepping between the thrashing wildcats, Loki wrestled the knife free and tossed it onto the table.

"What in the name of Helheim are you two doing?"

Sela skidded into Loki's boot. Instinctively, her arms hugged his leg seeking protection. Blue eyes darkened with animosity and confusion, glared at Laufey then up to Loki.

"Do something. Kill her. It's the witch from my dreams. She was the crazy healer outside my village. She wants to kill me and steal the baby," Sela screeched... not altogether coherently.

Laufey rose to her feet and dusted herself off.

Ignoring Sela's hysterical ranting, she plucked the scalpel from the table. Grumbling to herself about needing to clean it *again* and that the ignorant wench had better not have damaged the blade, she faced the couple.

Her words were sharp.

"If not for the fact, you are carrying my grandchild, I would kick you out of here to die in the fields, which I doubt my son would appreciate—"

The only word Sela registered was the one with which she interrupted Laufey, "Grandchild?"

"Yes, and if you don't let me do my job, then both you and baby will be dead in a matter of minutes. Now shut up and let me get to work."

Baffled, Sela angled her head to look at Loki.

He met her gaze and nodded in tacit acknowledgement of everything Laufey had said.

The adrenaline ebbed from Sela's system, to be replaced by unbearable pain.

"Get her on the mat, Loki, and hold her tight," Laufey barked orders. "We don't have time to knock her out and I can only hope the salve has taken effect."

Doing as instructed, Loki heaved Sela onto the furs, immobilising her arms against the floor. Laufey straddled Sela's legs and wedged a stick between the girl's teeth, telling her to bite hard.

Saying a small healing chant, she sliced into Sela's belly.

Her teeth clamping down on the stick, Sela cried out but, fighting for breath, passed out.

Laufey heaved a grateful sigh, although her concern was more for her granddaughter than the woman bleeding beneath her.

If she saved Sela, all well and good. If she died, it was not her problem.

At least she's no longer fighting me.

Loki was endlessly impressed by his mother's surgical skills. Fascinated, he watched Laufey make the incision, then slide her hand, inch by meticulous inch, through muscle and tissue to the womb. Tender fingers reached inside Sela and, adeptly, freed the cord from the baby's neck.

Slowly and carefully, Laufey extricated the infant from her mother's womb, then tied off the cord before cutting it.

A firm smack on the baby's bottom, coaxed a loud, healthy squall from her new granddaughter.

"The blanket." She nodded at Loki, who retrieved the soft woolen sheet.

Tears of joy flowed from the old woman's eyes as she swaddled the precious child, and settled the girl in her father's arms so she could tend to the mother.

Laufey's precision and dexterity with a needle would be envied by the finest seamstresses. Scarring was unavoidable but, unless one was looking for it, it would go unnoticed.

Laufey chuckled to herself when she tied the last knot; considering who the wench was married to, she would probably write it off as a dueling scar.

Gently smoothing a balm made from healing herbs, across the wound, to reduce the risk of poison, Laufey bandaged Sela's belly with strips of cloth, and left her on the furs to check on her granddaughter.

A tired smile warmed her face seeing Loki and the baby sharing a tender moment. The world's view of her son was limited to sagas and legends told by those who did not know him.

To be fair, he warranted most of the bad publicity, but this paternal facet of his character was witnessed by less than a handful of people... even if his offspring *did i*nclude the Mistress of Helheim, a great lolloping wolf, and that grotesque serpent who encircled the Earth just waiting for the day to devour it.

Laufey chalked *that* up to bad choices in women.

Relieving Loki of his daughter, Laufey laid the infant on the table to check her properly.

"Ten fingers, ten toes, a solid set of lungs, and a strong heartbeat."

Laufey sensed there was more to this child. It was nothing she could see, this was intangible; an innate power even greater than that of her father.

Keeping her intuition to herself, Laufey plastered a smile on her face, washed the child quickly, wrapped her in a clean blanket, and tucked her into a nest of furs alongside her mother.

Returning to Loki she spoke quietly as she wiped the remains of Sela's blood from her hands.

"You have a healthy daughter, Loki. She looks strong and beautiful. As for the Midgardian, she should recover quickly, nature willing."

Laufey hooked her arm through Loki's and escorted him out of the house.

"They need rest and you gawking at them won't help."

Outside, Loki crumpled onto a fallen log, his features strained.

Laufey sat next to him, her ancient hand engulfed in his. She sensed the loss of his energy, aware his fears for his child and wife had taken a toll.

She patted his hand and maintained her inscrutable façade.

Loki did not need her to say anything, the questions were already there. "I don't understand, Mother. Sela should be immortal; but she still almost died.

"How? And why was I unable to help her?"

Her eyes fixed on the ground Laufey explained, "Immortality is relative, child.

"In your woman's realm, age and death may not be able to touch her, but we both know anything possessing ancient powers can snuff her life out like a candle."

She paused, seeking the right words. Despite not finding the ones she wanted, she forged ahead.

"Had you not come to me, your child would have taken your woman's life. Your energy, while strong enough to bring them through the portal, lacks the potency to save your wife. Your daughter is the one, Loki, destined to end Odin's tyranny."

Laufey lifted her head, seeing a completely different scene from the bustling village in front of her, lamenting the mistake her realm had made eons ago. "We should never have given that Asgardian so much power. He didn't know how to control it and it has corrupted him. He is like a spoiled child with a dangerous toy."

Loki assumed a long-suffering expression. "Just once, I wish I could conceive a child who is not bent on destruction."

Amused by her son's remark, Laufey chuckled. "No, my little warrior, she's here to set the realms straight, and Odin knows there is nothing he can do to stop her.

"That's why the price on your woman was so high."

"Surely, they are safe here, aren't they? There is no way Odin can reach either of them in this realm," desperation laced his plea.

"Your daughter is safe here, but the same cannot be said for the mother. Her body might recover from the birth quickly but, as I mentioned, immortality is relative.

"Time in our realm will affect her adversely, even now it is preparing to attack, to desecrate her body. She does not belong here and possesses no ability to fight her true age."

It occurred to Laufey that she ought to check on Sela, which also gave her a good excuse to curtail this conversation, aware Loki was leading to the one question she didn't want to answer.

Rising from the log, she cupped her son's chin and studied each detail of his beautiful face as though she was never going to see him again.

"I need to monitor your woman, Loki. You stay here and rest," Laufey dropped a light kiss on his cheek.

As she turned, she heard Loki say. "Sela, her name is Sela."

The old woman smiled to herself at his words. It was obvious, after all these centuries, he had found a woman whom he could love without reserve.

Leaving him to ponder the future, she entered the dwelling.

Laufey came to a halt just inside the doorway. Mother and child were bonding for the first time. Sela was cradling her daughter, tears streaking down her cheeks as she rocked the newborn.

She cleared her throat to let Sela know she was there, and said, "She looks like her father."

"Nonsense," Sela contradicted. "She is the image of her grandmother."

While a blatant attempt to win over Laufey, the latter appreciated the gesture.

Blushing, Sela apologized for her earlier outburst, "I'm sorry I hit you."

Waving that off Laufey grinned, and rubbed her jaw which still throbbed dully. "Would take more than an errant blow from a puny Midgardian to do any permanent damage. How are you feeling?"

"I'm a little sore, but the surgeon did an excellent job of stitching and the cut looks almost healed.

"I am curious, though, should my milk have come in so quickly?" Sela quizzed.

Time was already accelerating.

Masking her true feelings, Laufey explained with grandmotherly reassurance, "The surgeon has a name. It is Laufey.

"As for your milk, it's natural in this place for things to happen at a faster pace than in your realm. I am sure you will be on your feet just as quickly.

"Now, let this healer inspect her work."

Nestling the baby next to her on the furs, Sela let Laufey examine her stitches.

"So, no calling you Granny or Gamma," Sela tested the waters.

"No, Laufey will do."

"Fine, Laufey it is. Can't guarantee your granddaughter will—"

The older woman's furrowed brow, arrested Sela's train of thought.

"Is something wrong?"

Schooling her features into a teasing smile, Laufey prevaricated, "No, I was thinking I should have stitched my name into your belly so you would have a reminder of me."

The pair shared a laugh, but Laufey was genuinely concerned because the incision had healed completely and the scar, which should have been more pronounced, was vanishing.

Loki needed to get his woman out of here with all haste.

Applying a clean bandage to conceal the truth, Laufey distracted Sela by propping her against a pile of pillows.

She placed the child in Sela's arms, suggesting, "See whether your daughter will nurse."

The baby required no coaxing, latching onto Sela's breast to suckle voraciously.

Sela watched in awe. *This is definitely Loki's child — her appetite matches that of her father.*

"Have you named her yet?" Laufey asked.

"No, your son can never be serious enough to help come up with one. The last one he threw out was Bjorgfrid. Really? Does he imagine I want my daughter named for combat?"

Sela giggled at the knowing smile of the old woman. "I

banned him from the baby book at that point. It could be worse, I suppose. He might have wanted to name her *Freya*," she bit out the name.

"Hush, child. Freya is his ancient past," Laufey soothed as she stroked her granddaughter's head. "It is obvious who holds his heart."

Sela brooded, "Perhaps someone should explain that to *her*."

Peace descended as the two watched the baby feed.

Eventually, unable to stay quiet, Sela broke the comfortable silence.

"We can't stay here, can we?"

"What makes you ask?" Laufey tried to maintain the pretense that nothing was amiss. "You need to heal and the child needs to gain—"

"Laufey, stop. I spent a millennia chained to a rock in Helheim because I believed somebody's lie, so I know what one sounds like. What's wrong?"

Without a word, the old woman got to her feet and stepped across the small space to her worktable, where she began amassing an assortment of supplies the family might need once they left this realm.

"Laufey?" Sela beseeched, and the woman's hands hovered, motionless, above a bundle of herbs.

Unwilling to repeat the scene she had outside with Loki, Laufey replied, "The thousand years you just spoke of will be upon you within a matter of days if you stay here, Sela. Your husband and your child will watch you wither and die.

"While keeping them here would warm my heart, it will kill Loki to see you take your last breath. So, yes, the three of you must leave here as quickly as possible."

"What about Odin and his damned bounty? I thought the whole reason Loki dragged us here was for protection?"

The futility of the situation was more than Sela could bear.

"Loki, *had* to bring you here, it was predestined, in the same way as Leif Ericksson was led to this place, to establish a portal between your realm and ours.

"It was done so your daughter could be born, but now you need to get back to your world before it's too late."

Laufey finished packing a medical kit of herbs and salve for the child. She included some dried fish and fruit.

The trio probably did not need it, but it made Laufey feel as though she had contributed to their safety, despite the fact that all she was doing was sending them away.

"Laufey, why does it fall on my child to save the realms? If Odin is so out of control, why don't the rest of you take care of him?"

Sela deemed this to be not only a legitimate question, but also a better solution.

"Because of Gungnir," Laufey's tone was devoid of emotion.

"Odin's *spear*?" This only added to Sela's confusion.

"Yes, my child, because of that wretched spear.

"It is the source of his power and makes him untouchable, even by us. It is imbued with the magic which created the realms and stars above, and it was Loki who gave it to him.

"Loki trusted that pestiferous Asgardian as you would trust a father, and convinced our elders that Odin was the right god to guide the other realms. We were no less foolish to believe."

Seeing her granddaughter sleeping peacefully in her mother's arms, Laufey changed topics.

"Now is not the time for long stories, Sela. You both should rest. You need to be ready to travel by morning."

Sela did feel sleepy, though she could not be sure whether the old healer was responsible or it was a natural after effect of childbirth.

Before slumber took her, she murmured, "I really want to call our daughter, Anna. It is an ancient name meaning beautiful and blessed with grace, but..."

Sela hesitated, uncharacteristically shy, her words beginning to slur, "...I think Anna Laufey has a certain flourish. Would you have any objections?"

As Sela drifted off to sleep, Laufey nodded with a smile.

"I would have done so if you *hadn't*."

TWELVE

The sunrise crept into the house like a thief sneaking across the floor. When it reached Sela, the light seemed to drill through her closed eyelids directly into her brain.

That searing sensation was a picnic compared with the excruciating pain that gripped her muscles and joints as she tried to raise her arms. It was as though the entire weight of time was crushing her to the floor.

As queen, Sela had witnessed men being drawn and quartered. The sounds of their ligaments snapping and tearing from the bone haunted her now as her own joints were ravaged.

To make matters worse, it felt as if every battle scar had suddenly torn open. Sela was sure her flesh was peeling from her body.

She understood what Laufey had been trying to explain the night before.

Sela tried to scream, but her lungs refused to emit anything more than a shallow moan. Breath, too, was becoming a fleeting luxury.

Death was at hand.

Fortunately for her, the baby felt it as well and gave vent to a wail which woke the house.

Fighting slumber, Loki muttered for Sela to feed the child before she disturbed the entire village. His words went unheeded and the baby's screams intensified.

With a groan, he opened his eyes and lifted up on one elbow to spot Laufey's booted foot about to kick his butt in an attempt to wake him.

"Loki, **get up**," Laufey screeched. "You need to get Sela out of here **now**."

There was no time for Laufey to elaborate, she spun on her heel to gather the pack she had prepared the night before, as well as her granddaughter, and bolted for the door.

Glancing back, she saw Loki, with infinite care, lift his wife from the furs.

Pained whimpers accompanied the wheeze of Sela's shallow breaths as Loki followed his mother. The group hurried to the portal to Midgard and Sela's own time.

Laufey feared they were too late to save her, but kept that to herself. Her son was a strong soul and would deal with the loss in his own way... meaning, uncontrolled destruction and revenge brought upon the realms under Odin's reign.

Without saying goodbye, Laufey kissed her granddaughter on the forehead and her son on the cheek.

Before Loki could utter a word, she whispered the chant to propel the family to the other side.

Looking up at the sky, seeing the moon suspended high above and surrounded by her glittering guardians, Loki knew time had not passed but a few seconds in this realm since they stepped through the portal.

He peered at Sela.

Her ashen face was illuminated by the silvery luminescence of Mani's orb.

Was she breathing? Loki was certain she had died during the transition.

Even their child was silent, as though already mourning the loss of her mother.

Loki placed Sela on the grassy mound, then dug through Laufey's satchel for anything to revive his wife.

Vial after vial proved worthless.

The mighty god's rage began to boil at his inability to save her.

"Damn you, Sela. Damn you to Helheim for leaving me," Loki hollered helplessly at the night sky.

"Really, Loki, you sound like an old woman," the voice startled Loki into silence, but he knew who it was without having to look.

"Shut the fuck up, Freya. If anybody knows what an old woman sounds like, it's you." Loki scowled over his shoulder.

"My, she even has you talking like her. I did not realize how much power our friend there has over you."

Loki felt Freya's presence strengthen as he prepared himself to kill her. Sela would want him to and, right now, it was the only way to honor his lost woman.

Hearing the whisper of grass being flattened underfoot, he spun to attack. Snarling and baring his fangs, he lunged.

Nonchalantly, the goddess raised her palm and froze him in his tracks.

"Your anger will be your undoing, Loki. If you want her dead, go ahead and strike me down. If you do, her death is on *you*. That said, given you destroyed the fae I had sent to rescue the pair of you, the more I think about it... the less I'm inclined to think she's worth saving."

Freya brushed her hand over Loki's chest as she passed him. "Good help is so hard to find, you know."

Kneeling next to Sela, Freya began to examine her erstwhile rival.

"Fate did her no favors by forcing you to bring her here, but I think there may be hope."

Loki attempted to reel in his temper by asking a related question.

"How did you know where we were, Freya? There was no way you should have been able to track us. I didn't even let Sela know where we were going until I had no choice. It was the only way I could be sure you wouldn't be able to search her mind."

Freya shrugged, pausing momentarily. "Now why would I do that?"

She looked up at the god she once thought would be her toy forever.

"It was your child who led me here. Seems she knew I was going to be needed, even if you didn't."

She returned to her duties, reciting an incantation.

A translucent radiance began to replace the pallor of Sela's flesh.

The louder the chants, the brighter Sela became. Her body levitated until she was suspended above Freya.

Positive this would garner the attention of the park rangers, Loki kept one eye on their shack.

Sela's body bowed upwards as the cool night air filled

her lungs. Imbued with the magic consuming her, Sela's eyes fluttered open.

The scream, trapped within her at Laufey's home, was unlocked and pealed through the darkness.

Satisfied with her handiwork, Freya let Sela plummet, unceremoniously, to the ground.

The thud of the younger woman hitting the hardened mud brought a chuckle from Freya.

"Bitch," Sela growled at the goddess as she lay sprawled on the ground, trying to collect herself.

"Is that anyway to thank me for saving your life? Talk about ungrateful." Freya smiled angelically.

"Besides, I was pretty sure the fall wouldn't kill you."

Rising to her feet, Sela rubbed her backside, hissing, "If anyone around here deserves to be killed it's *you*."

"Oh, come now, Sela. I've been chasing you across Canada in a bid to help you. Don't make me regret indulging your child's petition... even if she did more or less compel me to oblige."

"You've been chasing us? Wait... *Anna* summoned you? How?" Sela didn't know which revelation startled her more... *No, it was definitely the latter.*

"Don't you think I might have noticed a chariot pulled by cats following me?"

"Hon, welcome to the twenty-first century. I got tired of trying to corral those damn felines. The only cat to transport me now is my '70 Cougar.

"More power and a *much* better air conditioner. If you had stopped long—"

Abruptly, several things coalesced in Sela's brain.

The image of a black and blue Mercury Cougar stuck in a snowdrift, the similar car on the ferry... that damn waitress and her freaky note.

Sela snagged a handful of Freya's hair, wanting to free the witch of it.

This woman... grrrrr.

Testily, she shoved aside the realization. There was no time to dwell on the scheming antics of the weather-bitten crone, and it was too late to chastise herself for mistakes, she could not undo... a far more crucial revelation required clarifying.

Still clutching Freya's hair, Sela demanded, "How did *Anna* compel you? She's scarcely twelve hours old. I don't understand any of this?"

Sela was perturbed to discover her unborn child had been in constant contact with the very deity, she had, thus far, trusted the least.

Unsnarling Sela's fingers from her tresses, Freya attempted to employ a weapon the Norse Deity seldom resorted to... logic.

"There's no time to explain. Unless you wish to enlighten the local constabulary as to why you are trespassing on national park land solely to give birth. Otherwise, I would recommend you release your grip and take a step back so we all make for the gate."

Sela's reply was drowned out by the wail of sirens and the rumble of jeeps approaching the grassy mound.

The group could see the pulsing red and blue growing brighter.

"You better hurry and make your choice, girl," Freya advised. "Seems your banshee howl already alerted them."

Anna was thrust into Sela's arms, as Loki hoisted her up in his own.

Sela caught a glimpse of Freya disappearing into the darkness, hightailing it for the parking lot.

Sela curled against Loki's chest, doing her best to protect the baby and not fall from his arms.

A brilliant flash of light brought the world to a standstill.

CHAPTER

THIRTEEN

Sela felt Loki tighten his hold as he skidded to a halt.

The thunderous voice of Odin shattered the night as he confronted Freya. "I should have known I'd find you in the middle of this, Freya. Your treachery has come to an end."

"Oh, Mighty Odin, praise you for your timely appearance. I was afraid they would escape before you found us."

The goddess sounded so convincing, Sela shouted, "I should have stabbed you when I had the chance, Freya."

Freya yelled back, "Silence, whore. You have had this coming for a long time—"

Sela freed herself from Loki's arms and, baby in tow, charged at Freya, screaming, "*I'm* a whore? That's rich. Who's been sleeping with *my* husband for eons? Right under this idiot's nose, no less." Sela gesticulated in Odin's general direction.

The pair went toe to toe, hurling insults and accusations at each other.

His eyes spitting fire, Odin glowered at the two women, their shrill voices giving him a headache.

Freya spun away from Sela to face Odin, professing her innocence, and affirming her dedication to him. "Surely, you see everything I have done was for you, Odin. Do not believe a word that trips off the forked tongue of this hellion."

"Ha, that's rich coming from you, Freya," Sela countered and, with an angry flick of her hand, goaded, "Go on, inundate the crazy jackass with more rubbish. You certainly deluded him into believing Baldr is his son. God of all? Pah, more like a gullible old fool."

Going so far as to throw an additional slur at Freya for good measure, "Slut."

It may not have been Shakespearean but, damn, it felt good to say it.

Their screeched invective ruptured the thin threads tying Odin to his sanity. Pain hammered through his skull at their ceaseless howling until he could stand no more.

"Enough," he boomed. "I'll take care of you after—"

That's when the ruler of Valhalla realized he had taken his eye off Loki. *If it wasn't those traitorous valkyiries trying to usurp him, it was this bastarður. Was no one to be trusted?*

He swiveled to where Loki had been standing, to see nothing but darkness.

Without warning, a massive arm hooked around Odin's neck from behind, crushing his throat.

Odin struggled to free himself from Loki's grip, swinging his mighty fist blindly, hoping to dislodge his captor.

As the two deities locked horns, Loki yelled to Freya, "Get Sela and the baby out of here, ***now***."

Rather than waste his energy punching thin air, Odin jerked his head into Loki's face. His aim was true, and Loki's grip slackened momentarily.

He tried to dodge Odin's thrashing skull, but the old man's neck was like rubber and rotated at random. No matter how often Loki ducked, Odin landed blow after blow.

Freya, aware Odin was gaining the advantage, clutched Sela's arm, and tried to tug the younger woman towards her car.

Sela had other ideas. "No, my love, I can't leave you here. He's determined to kill you. I can help."

"Sela, I need to know you're safe. *Please* go with Freya," Loki entreated, feeling his chokehold weakening.

Freya yanked on Sela's arm for all she was worth, nearly tearing it from the shoulder, in her desperation to get her to move. They had mere seconds before the inevitable occurred.

Odin rammed his spear into the earth.

An explosion of soil and rock erupted into the sky.

Loki fell backwards, losing sight of the women as a curtain of dirt descended around them.

His attempt to leap to his feet, to block Odin from attacking them further, was thwarted — pinned to the ground by the point of Odin's spear.

Blood gushed from the wound as Odin plunged it deeper into Loki's stomach.

The Asgardian, Loki had once considered his closest friend, laughed manically at the sight. He twisted the blade, putting his weight against it burying it into his victim's body.

Summoning the last of his strength, Loki grabbed the mahogany shaft protruding from his gut, streaks of his blood marring the high polish.

With an abrupt flick of his wrist, he snapped it, tiny splinters spraying out around Odin's hands.

The crazed god's eyes widened in disbelief.

Odin vanished.

The din of supernatural battle was supplanted by the harsh engines of the rangers' jeeps prowling the park.

Try as he might, Loki could not see or hear any trace of Sela or Freya.

In vain, he wrenched at the spear, but it refused to be uprooted from the ground beneath him.

Death stalked him.

His gaze swung from the bloody wound sapping his essence, to the stars above.

Instead of the twinkling lights of his ancestors, he saw the smug glint in his daughter's eyes, as she stood over him, hands on hips.

"You wouldn't listen to me, would you? I *told* you she would be your downfall," Hel lectured dryly. "Glad she got what was coming to her."

Loki gaped at her, slack-jawed, desperate denials clawing at his throat as his physical form faded. "No... she can't be... you're wrong... I'm sure... they... go..."

Growing still and silent, Loki released his last breath, which rolled as mist into the night.

As far as Hel was concerned, her father's time in Midgard had come to a merciful conclusion.

Tending to Loki's remains, Hel knew she had much to do before she could take him home to Helheim. Worrying about the doom awaiting Sela and Freya was not part of it.

Hel swore that if she could save him, Loki would never learn of their fate.

"Those two interfering harpies have caused you enough pain, Father. Upon my oath, you shall never know suffering again."

Cradling Loki's limp body, Hel rose to her feet.

When the rangers appeared on scene, there was nobody to be seen, leaving them no alternative but to attribute the unearthly scream, splinters of wood, and disturbance of dirt to some weird natural phenomenon.

Blissfully unaware of the chaos conceived.

ODIN'S BANE SYNOPSIS
THE SELA HELSDATTER SAGA

Book Three

Sela Helsdatter cannot catch a break. Relentless in his jealousy and wrath, Odin is determined that neither Sela nor her infant daughter will survive.

Shattered by loss, and with no time to grieve, Sela has to rely on the one person she believes responsible for her current predicament.

A lost friendship is revived, and the disparate trio seek refuge in a remote corner of Montana, with the uneasy awareness the child may be the key to their salvation.

Vowing Odin will not harm a hair on her daughter's head, Sela has to use every trick at her disposal to thwart the Norse Deity. At the same time another fiendish subversion threatens the future of humanity.

A hunting trip sparks a chain of events, culminating in a confrontation in a cave at the centre of the world.

Will Odin be victorious, or is another power stirring which will prove to be his bane?

About the Author
RORI BLEU

With a smattering of riverboat pirates and royalty in her heritage, Rori Bleu's childhood reflected her past.
An interest in fairy tales, myth and legend were as important as spirited discussions around politics and current affairs — although some might argue they are one and the same!

A fascination, sparked by listening to Grimm's Fairy Tales at her grandmother's knee, not only encouraged Rori's passion for reading, but also steered her into the world of RPG's.
What began as a fun pastime, soon evolved into the creation of fantastical worlds, but Rori never lost her love of politics going on to specialise in Governmental History and Historical Research.

Naturally this means her stories are steeped in historical accuracy and real-life intrigue. While Rori's love of a happily ever after means her preferred genre is romance, don't be surprised if you discover an occasional detour into historical fiction, thrillers, horror and fantasy.

To find more of Rori's books... click the link
https://linktr.ee/roribleu

About the Author
ROSIE CHAPEL

Rosie Chapel lives in Perth, Australia with her hubby and two furkids. When not writing, she loves catching up with friends, burying herself in a book (or three), discovering the wonders of Western Australia, or — and the best — a quiet evening at home with her husband, enjoying a glass of wine and a movie.

Website: www.rosiechapel.com

ALSO BY RORI BLEU

Pineapple Meringue

Imprisoned Hearts

Port of London

Dani's Masquerade

Black Tulips

Ajei's Destiny

Porta Aeternum

The Queen's Heart

Syn *with Matthew Forester*

Echoes and Illusions *with Rosie Chapel*

Evie's War *with Rosie Chapel*

Vindicta *with Rosie Chapel*

The Sela Helsdatter Saga - with Rosie Chapel

A Flip of The Coin - Book One

Conceived Chaos - Book Two

Odin's Bane - Book Three

Also by Rosie Chapel

Of Ruins and Romance

All At Once It's You

Cobweb Dreams

Just One Step

His Heart's Second Sigh

<u>Dystopian Romance</u>

Echoes & Illusions *with Rori Bleu*